D1100034

AN OFFER OF MARRIAGE

It is 1892 and Lizzie Flintoff lives with her parents behind a small shop in Whitby, where her father makes and sells jewellery in the famous Whitby jet. However, the business is failing. Then the owner of the property tells them he wishes to sell it to someone for a bakery, and the Flintoffs must leave. They arrange to share a relative's cottage but, unfortunately, there is no room for Lizzie. When the elderly man Lizzie has always called 'Uncle Jack' says he is willing to marry her, she is faced with a heart-rending decision . . .

GILLIAN KAYE

AN OFFER OF MARRIAGE

Complete and Unabridged

LINFORD
Leicester

First published in Great Britain in 2004

First Linford Edition
published 2005

British Library CIP Data

Kaye, Gillian
    An offer of marriage.—Large print ed.—
Linford romance library
    1. Love stories
    2. Large type books
    I. Title
    823.9'14 [F]

    ISBN 1–84395–792–2

Published by
F. A. Thorpe (Publishing)
Anstey, Leicestershire

Set by Words & Graphics Ltd.
Anstey, Leicestershire
Printed and bound in Great Britain by
T. J. International Ltd., Padstow, Cornwall

This book is printed on acid-free paper

1

'Hush, Violet, there's no need to cry like that. Lizzie will hear you.' The man's voice was loud and clear.

'How can I help it, Josh, when you tell me such dreadful news?' The tearful reply came from his wife.

'There's worse to come I can tell you.' Words which were shouted back almost angrily.

In the next room, Lizzie sat bewildered.

It was a Sunday afternoon in the fishing-port of Whitby in 1892 and Lizzie Flintoff found herself listening to sounds which were to change her life for ever.

It was a very wet afternoon, and for June the rain was heavy. She could hear it against the windows of the living-room at the back of the house, and heaviest of all as it hit the slates of the outhouse across the back yard.

But the noise of the rain was comforting when she found that she was almost frightened by the sounds of her parents' voices reaching her from the shop.

Flintoff's was a respectable jewellers in narrow, cobbled Church Street; Mr Flintoff was a skilled craftsman of the famous Whitby jet, and the pieces of jewellery he fashioned were made in his workshop which opened straight out of the shop. Behind the shop and workshop was the large living-room where Lizzie was sitting with a quaking heart; alongside it was the kitchen where they cooked and ate their meals.

Had it been a fine afternoon, Mr and Mrs Flintoff and Lizzie might have taken a walk around the harbour and called to see Mary, who was their eldest child and Lizzie's only sister. In winter and in poor weather, Sunday afternoon would have found them all in the living-room. Mrs Flintoff and Lizzie were busy threading the small carved jet beads into necklaces, and Mr Flintoff dozing over his Sunday paper.

But this particular afternoon was different, and Lizzie sat at the table, the small black beads untouched in front of her. She could not be described as being a pretty girl, her face was long, her expression usually serious; but she had fine blue eyes and her mouth was generously shaped. When she smiled, she could be called good-looking.

She was twenty-three years of age, devoted to her parents and to being in charge of the shop which sold the beautiful jet necklaces, brooches and pendants which came from her father's skilled hands.

In all of those twenty-three years, Lizzie had never seen her mother in tears, she had never heard her father lose his temper. She knew that something must be very wrong for the two of them to be in the shop at all on a Sunday afternoon.

She listened intently, but they had dropped their voices and her mother's sobbing had ceased.

Still the voices raised in argument went on in the shop; she crept to the door and tried to listen. All she could hear were her father's steady tones, no longer raised in anger and then a frightened little scream from Mrs Flintoff. 'We can't do it, Joshua,' or 'Oh no, not that.'

Lizzie sat down at the table again and her fingers touched the beads; she could feel the fine raised pattern so finely worked by her father. But she did not have the heart to string them for she thought that this strange argument between her mother and father could mean only one thing. The shop must close.

Lizzie thought of the twenty years she could remember in Whitby. How the jet had become fashionable when the Queen had gone into black after Prince Albert had died. Even before that, Whitby jet had been valuable for Lizzie, as she knew that it had been shown at the Great Exhibition of 1851.

But now, the century was coming to its close and fashion was changing. After the Golden Jubilee in 1887, Queen Victoria had relaxed her strict mourning and ladies turned to lighter and brighter colours. Lizzie knew that she had to admit to herself that trade in the shop had been very quiet, and that many shops had closed.

Restlessly, she wandered through into the kitchen, filled the kettle and put it on the range; if her mother was upset, then she would be glad of some tea, Lizzie told herself.

It was four o'clock by the grandfather clock in the living-room when the door opened and her parents appeared. Afterwards, Lizzie thought that she would always remember the time, date and year. Four o'clock, on Sunday, June 5, 1892.

She stood at the table and watched her mother walk towards her, arms outstretched.

'My dear Lizzie,' Mrs Flintoff's voice was shaky, her eyes were red from crying, but still she looked a handsome woman. Taller than Lizzie and broad-shouldered, she could easily have been domineering, but Lizzie had never known her anything but kindly.

'What is going on, Mother?' Lizzie asked uncertainly, then turned to her father. 'I heard you shouting, Papa, that is not like you.'

Mr Flintoff was a serious man, very tall and with white hair; he was of sturdy build and always held himself upright.

'I'm sorry, Lizzie. I was trying to stop your mother from upsetting you. I regret to say that we have some very bad news for you.'

'Not from Hartlepool?' Lizzie asked anxiously.

'No, your brothers are well out of it, thank the good Lord.' Mr Flintoff sat down heavily at the table, his head buried in his hands.

Lizzie walked towards the kitchen. 'Sit down, Mother. I put the kettle on a little while back. We'll have some tea.'

Lizzie busied herself with getting the tea, quite unable to imagine what catastrophe could have befallen them.

Mr Flintoff explained at length and very carefully. 'Lizzie, you are in the shop enough to know that business has fallen off badly. You may not have realised that I am doing very little work and there are no new orders coming in.'

Her mother was sitting very quietly, she seemed lost in her own thoughts. 'I think we might have weathered the storm, Lizzie, but yesterday brought bad news,' her father told her.

'Was it to do with Mr Weatherill coming?' Lizzie asked.

Mr Weatherill owned the Flintoff's property and he had always been a fair and reasonable landlord.

'Yes, I'm afraid so. He is not getting any younger and he has had a good offer for these premises from someone who wants to open up a bakery.'

Lizzie stared. She heard a sob from her mother. 'A bakery?' she echoed unbelievingly. 'You mean to take out the workshop and put ovens in?'

'Yes, I'm afraid that's correct,' said Mr Flintoff soberly.

'But, Papa, you have lived here all these years. It was Grandad who taught you the craft of jet, and you took it over when he died. Mr Weatherill cannot turn you out just like that.'

'I'm afraid he can, Lizzie. I can't complain because the rent has been very reasonable and we did very well until the trade started to decline. This last year, it's been a struggle to find the rent.'

'You didn't tell me, Papa,' Lizzie said reproachfully.

'I kept hoping that it would improve, my dear, but it was just the opposite. Then they started bringing in soft jet from France and Spain. People bought it because it was cheap, but then they took against the foreign stuff because it cracked so quickly. Good Whitby jet doesn't do that, but it was too late. It all affected the genuine trade.'

Lizzie could hardly believe what she

was hearing, no wonder she had heard her mother crying. She struggled with ideas and looked at her father. 'Papa, couldn't you buy the premises from Mr Weatherill and we could turn it into a nice house for ourselves?'

He looked sorrowful. 'I'm sorry, Lizzie, there is no money. I'm already in debt to Mr Weatherill for several months rent, he has been very forbearing.'

Lizzie looked at him with consternation. This was getting worse and worse, and they had kept it from her as though she had been a little girl.

'How long have we got, Papa?'

'Until the end of next week.'

'But that is no time at all,' Her voice was shrill. 'What are you going to do?'

Her father was more serious than ever. Lizzie looked at her mother. There were tears rolling down her cheeks and she was feeble with dabbing them with a handkerchief.

'Papa?'

'Your mother and I are going to live

with your Uncle George. He has agreed to take me on.'

Lizzie stood up then, she felt herself getting both angry and scared. 'But Uncle George is a fisherman.'

'Lizzie,' her father roared at her. 'A man is not to be despised because he is a fisherman. It is an honourable calling. Please do not forget that Our Lord's first disciples were fishermen.'

She knew that her father would have mentioned his strong beliefs only in very serious circumstances. He was a devout man and attended chapel, but his religion was a private matter to him.

'Yes, Papa,' Lizzie said in a small voice. She knew that he was right. Then she thought of her Uncle George and Aunt Cathy whom she loved, George being her father's older brother. They lived in a tiny cottage in Cliff Street, Uncle George had been a fisherman all his life and worked hard. They had brought up two sons and two daughters in that small cottage, Lizzie's cousins were now all married and living elsewhere in the town. Then her thoughts became words as the significance of her father's words became clear to her.

'What about me?' she asked and hoped that her voice did not sound as frightened as she felt. 'Uncle George has only the two bedrooms, all my cousins had to share the same room even though they were brothers and sisters. But I never did hear them grumble.' Her voice faltered. 'Do you mean me to share the second bedroom with you, Mother?'

Mrs Flintoff leaned over the table and took her daughter's hand. 'It is terrible business, Lizzie, but we think that it is the only thing we can do. George has been very kind, he is older than your father, but he has his own fishing boat and is willing to take Joshua on. It is our good fortune that one of your cousins is buying his own boat so that it is possible for your father to take his place.'

She gave Lizzie's hand a squeeze.

'My dear, we would not expect you to share a small bedroom in George's cottage with us. It would be neither seemly nor comfortable. You are a young lady now. Your father will tell you what he has been able to arrange for you and I hope that you will be pleased with his efforts on your behalf.'

Something in her mother's voice made Lizzie suspicious. They have made plans without telling me in case something like this should happen, she told herself. My mother is not sure how I will receive their suggestion, I can tell by her voice. Then she took heed as her father started to speak.

'My dear Elizabeth,' he began and immediately Lizzie was on her guard. Her full name was used only in the gravest of circumstances. 'You will no doubt remember that a few weeks ago, we enjoyed a visit from my great friend, James Wilkes, always known to you as Uncle Jack. Not because he is a relative of ours, but because he has been a close friend all my life.'

12

'What has Uncle Jack to do with it all?' asked Lizzie with some curiosity dispelling her uneasy feelings. She had always loved her Uncle Jack whom she thought of as kind and jolly, and whom she knew had a particular fondness for her.

'As you know, James lives in Glaisdale, and Pexton House is a very fine house and estate. You also know that his dear wife, Rhoda, died six months ago leaving him with Amelia and young James, whom we know as Jimmy. They are growing up fast, Amelia is now eighteen and Jimmy is seventeen.'

'Why are you telling me all this? I am well-acquainted with Melia — as we've always called her — and Jimmy.' Lizzie was beginning to feel puzzled.

'James told me a few weeks ago that he hoped to marry again, he finds it lonely without Rhoda. And he has confided in me that if anything ever happened to Rhoda, it was his dearest wish to be able to ask you to be his wife. I went to see him yesterday and he is still of the same mind and that if the match pleases you, he will come into Whitby this week to see you and to make you an offer of marriage.

'He wishes to make the arrangements for your wedding and your removal to Pexton House so that there will be no need for you to have to think about living with us in George's cottage . . . why, what is it, Lizzie? I thought you would feel honoured at such a good opportunity of becoming the wife of the owner of Pexton House . . . Elizabeth . . . '

Lizzie jumped up, her cheeks scarlet, facing him across the table.

'How dare you, how dare you. Promise me to a man only a little younger than yourself, a man who has always been as an uncle to me. What are you thinking of? Marry Uncle Jack? Of course I cannot marry Uncle Jack and I am not even going to stay here and discuss it with you as a dutiful daughter should.'

Lizzie snatched up a shawl and

rushed through the shop into the street; this to the sound of her mother's wail.

'The rain, Lizzie, the rain.'

But Lizzie did not care about the rain. She put her shawl over her head and ran up Church Street, across Kiln Yard and then down Church Stairs, which linked the church of St. Mary with Henrietta Street and the sea.

Marry Uncle Jack? Marry a man old enough to be her father? She loved Uncle Jack, he was the kindest of gentleman, but marriage? Never, her heart cried out, never. How could I marry Uncle Jack when I still grieve over Geoffrey?

And for a few moments, she was back in the past. Two years ago when she had fallen in love with Geoffrey Herriot, a young school-teacher in Whitby. Handsome, smiling, full of flattery and fun, she had met him at the New Chapel in Baxtergate which the Flintoff family had always attended.

Geoffrey had loved her, too, or so she had thought. That was until, three weeks before their wedding, he had told her — and not very sorrowfully — that he was leaving Whitby and going back to his home in Middlesborough where he hoped to marry his childhood sweetheart, Ruth. It was only as his wedding to Lizzie drew near that he realised that it was Ruth he still loved and that he intended to keep the vow he had made to her when he had left home.

For a whole year, Lizzie had been tearful and angry in turn, until her sister, Mary, and her mother made her realise that she was better off without the fickle Geoffrey.

As she set foot on the last of the Church Stairs, she was in the present again, near to Mary's house in Henrietta Street, and the opportunity of sharing her awful prospect with her sister.

Mary Dodgson was thirty years of age and happily married to Henry, a Whitby fisherman. Their children were two mischievous and energetic boys of eight and ten years of age. Mary and Henry had suffered the loss of two little girls who had died when no more than babies.

Lizzie reached their cottage, rather hoping that the boys would not be at home and that she could have Mary to herself. And it was Mary who opened he door and smiled when she saw Lizzie, then realising that something was wrong, became concerned.

'Luckily the boys are down at the harbour with Henry. We can be quiet for once. Tell me everything,' Mary said. She was as tall and dark as Lizzie, and it was always obvious to strangers that they were sisters.

Lizzie related the conversation with their mother and father and Mary remained quiet and serious throughout, once or twice putting out a hand to Lizzie's with a comforting touch.

When it came to the end, Lizzie had difficulty in finding the right words. 'Uncle Jack, Mary, our dear Uncle Jack, you know we have always loved him though he's not related to us. He wants to marry me . . . oh Mary, Papa is so pleased, but I can see that Mother is upset. You can't marry a man you have always thought of as an uncle, can you? I am so upset and please tell me that you agree with me. Please, Mary.'

Mary got up from her chair and went to Lizzie, putting an arm around her. 'Of course you cannot marry a man of Uncle Jack's age. What is Papa thinking of?' She bent and gave Lizzie a kiss. 'I do think that he is trying to do his best for you, Lizzie. It must have been like a lifeline to him when Uncle Jack made his offer of marriage. He didn't think of your feelings. Does he know what you think of the idea?'

Lizzie shook her head. 'I was very angry and very rude and he will never forgive me. I shouted at him and ran out into the rain and came straight here.'

'I can understand how you feel about Uncle Jack, Lizzie, but have you really considered it properly? He is a man of property and ample fortune, you would have a good life as Mrs James Wilkes. What is there against him?'

'He is so old, Mary,' Lizzie protested.

'He does not look as old as he is for he is quite handsome and jolly. He has had a sad time, too, when you think of it.'

'Until he married Aunt Rhoda and inherited Pexton House.'

Mary nodded. 'Yes, but before that when he was learning to be a jet carver in Papa's workshop. He married when he was only eighteen and Cecily died giving birth to their little boy. Do you remember Stephen when he was older and you were a little girl, he used to chase us up and down Church Stairs?'

Lizzie smiled, suddenly diverted by the memory. 'I hated him, he pulled my hair and called me 'Sprat' because I was so small. Then when Uncle Jack married again and Melia and Jimmy were born, we didn't see them quite so much, though I did like going on the train to visit them. Stephen left home years ago, but Melia and Jimmy are still at Pexton House.

Lizzie looked at her sister suspiciously. 'Are you trying to persuade me that it would be a good thing to marry Uncle Jack?' she asked, none too graciously.

Mary shook her head. 'No, I don't think that it is right. But I have an idea.'

'I hope it is a good one,' snapped Lizzie.

'It's like this, Lizzie. The shop is closing down, you cannot very well live with Uncle George and I'm afraid we haven't a spare room here or you would be welcome. I do not agree with you marrying Uncle Jack, but why don't you offer to go to Pexton House as his housekeeper?'

2

In the tiny cottage in Henrietta Street, Lizzie stared at her sister. 'Become Uncle Jack's housekeeper? Whatever will you think of next, Mary? I never heard such a ridiculous notion.'

Mary grinned, for she was not offended by Lizzie's words. 'Work it out, Lizzie. Uncle Jack has been on his own for six months. Pexton House is a large mansion, you know that, and it needs someone to run it. Aunt Rhoda was always very efficient and I expect everything has been left to Cook all this time . . . I don't seem to remember Cook's name . . . '

Lizzie interrupted with a smile. 'Mrs Hamlyn. When we were smaller, we used to roll out pastry biscuits in that big kitchen. Do you remember?'

Mary nodded. 'It will have been hard for Mrs Hamlyn to be doing all the cooking and running the house at the same time. It is no wonder that Uncle Jack wishes to marry again.'

'But it doesn't have to be to me,' replied Lizzie bluntly.

'No, that is precisely my meaning. Uncle Jack might be quite happy to have you there as his housekeeper. You don't have to be his wife.' She stopped as she saw a faltering look on Lizzie's face. 'Think of how we always loved going to Glaisdale End and walking up the dale to Pexton House.'

Lizzie nodded for Mary's words had struck a chord in her memory.

Mary's voice brought her back into the present. 'You are remembering how lovely it was, Lizzie,' she said gently.

'Yes, you're right. They were happy times and I've remembered something else, too. I was about thirteen or fourteen years old and we were all in that wood on the other side of the bank. It was just before Stephen went off to Oxford and he chased me round the trees and when he caught me, he kissed me.' She gave a chuckle. 'Uncle Jack has said that he's settled in York. I expect he's married by now, though I don't remember Uncle Jack saying anything about it. Do you know, Mary, I have a feeling that there was a quarrel between them, though I never knew why. Uncle Jack rarely mentions Stephen these days.'

'I remember something Mother said once,' replied Mary. 'Uncle Jack wanted Stephen to marry the daughter of a neighbour of theirs, but she was older than Stephen and he refused. I think that is why he settled in York.'

'Perhaps she would do for Uncle Jack.' Lizzie laughed. 'If I go there, I must make enquiries.'

Mary looked at her. 'You're considering the idea,' she said quietly.

Lizzie nodded. 'Yes, I suppose I must be. I could easily run a house such as that, and I would have Melia for company, and Jimmy, of course. But we don't know if Uncle Jack would agree to it, do we?'

'Talk it over with Mother and Papa. See what they think.'

Lizzie got up and gave Mary a kiss. 'You're a good sister to me. I'll walk slowly up Church Stairs and think it over. By the time I reach the top — I believe they say that there are 199 stairs — I might have made up my mind. Thank you, Mary.'

'Come back and see me when Uncle Jack has been, won't you? And tell Papa that I am very sorry about the business, I cannot imagine it as a bakery.'

As she returned to the shop and entered the living-room, her mother looked relieved and reproachful at the same time.

'Where have you been all this time, Lizzie, and your dress must be wet through. Run upstairs and change into a dry one and bring the wet one down to dry by the fire.'

'I went to see Mary, Mother, she was very kind. I cannot marry Uncle Jack, you must see that, and Mary understands. She had an idea.'

'Did she? And what was that?'

'That I should go to Pexton House, but as Uncle Jack's housekeeper, not as his wife.' Lizzie spoke quite calmly.

'His housekeeper? But, my dear girl, Uncle Jack wants you for a wife.'

'Then he will be disappointed, Mother. I am not going to marry someone who is more than twice my age.'

'But Uncle Jack is so kind, Lizzie, he would make you a good husband.' Mrs Flintoff sounded flustered.

'He can be just as kind to me if I am his housekeeper. And it would be nice for Melia to have someone young in the house.'

Mrs Flintoff sighed. 'I believe perhaps you're right, my dear. We don't wish to force you into a marriage which is distasteful to you. We'll tell your father and then we must wait and see what Uncle Jack has to say when he comes.'

There was no time to be lost and it was sad to see the workshop dismantled on the first day. Then there was the stock of jet and jewellery and ornaments in the shop to be considered. Lizzie thought many times that she was going to burst into tears, but her father was stern and kindly at the same time and faced up to the loss of his lifetime's work with fortitude. Their favourite pieces of jet were given to family and friends; a few treasured and beautiful pieces which had never been for sale, were sent to the Whitby Museum.

On the day that they were trying to decide what to do with their furniture and all three of them were standing forlornly in the living-room, Mr James Wilkes arrived. He had to knock on the door of the shop, which was now closed and locked, and Mr Flintoff hurried to let him in.

'Jack, my dear fellow, you are very welcome, but you find us in sad disarray. Come through into the living-room.'

Lizzie felt nervous as she watched her uncle walk through the shop. Then at the same time, she had a sense of surprise. A pleasant surprise.

James Wilkes was forty-seven years of age and looked younger. His dark hair showed not a trace of grey and it was worn short and brushed back.

He kissed Mrs Flintoff and expressed his regret at their misfortune, then turned to Lizzie with a smile.

'My dearest Lizzie, give me your hands. This is a hard time for you, and you will know by now that I would like to help you out of your difficulties.'

He pressed Lizzie's hands briefly and she sat down, thankful that he had not been more effusive.

'My father has told me of your proposal, Uncle Jack,' she said in an outright manner. She noticed that her father had taken Mrs Flintoff back into the shop and she was left on her own with her suitor.

'He has? That's good. It has given you time to think it over. But first of all, Lizzie, I must tell you that the offer of marriage has come out of my sincere affection for you. I am a wealthy man, I have a nice home, but these last months have been lonely ones. I kept thinking of you and how you had always been a favourite with me. Lizzie is on her own, I am on my own, I said to myself. What could be nicer than to have her as my wife? And so I approached your father and he made no objection. So here I am. I ask you outright, Lizzie, will you marry me?'

Lizzie felt bewildered. Here was her favourite uncle looking younger than she had remembered. He was kind, she was fond of him. Was it just his age that made her hesitate? And she knew the answer to her own question. She had loved once and had lost her love, but she had known the joy of it and knew now that she could never marry anyone whom she did not love very much indeed.

Young ladies did marry to please their families, she knew that, but she also knew that often those marriages were not happy ones.

'Uncle Jack,' she said quietly and carefully. 'I do indeed thank you for your kind offer, but I regret to say that I must turn it down. It's good of you to think of me at this dreadful time, but I cannot marry you.'

'Cannot marry me?' his voice was raised, his colour heightened. 'But I am doing you a great honour, Lizzie. I thought you would be delighted at the chance of being Mrs James Wilkes and mistress of Pexton House. I know you're fond of me.'

'Uncle Jack, I am only twenty-three and I think of you and Father as being the same age — no, let me finish. It's not right, and although I have always had a fondness for you, it is not enough in a marriage. When I marry, I want to love my husband.'

'Fine words, Lizzie, fine words, and I am not going to take your refusal as final. Two weeks in a crowded fisherman's cottage and you will be pleased to come running to Glaisdale.'

'Uncle Jack, that is unkind of you.

My Uncle George has been very good to Father and I honour him for it.' She stopped and wondered if it was the time to put her proposal to him. 'I have thought about it very seriously, Uncle Jack, and I wish to make a suggestion.'

'Go on.'

'I would be prepared to come to Pexton House to live, but it would not be as your wife. Would you be prepared to accept me as your housekeeper?'

Housekeeper. James Wilkes was thinking fast. She is a good girl and I do believe that if she came as my housekeeper that within a month, she would be prepared to become my wife. Why not?

'Housekeeper?' he said aloud. 'Well, that is an idea. It's true that I need a wife to see to the running of the house, it is too much for Cook. And you might like it so much at Pexton House, you may change your mind in a few months.'

Lizzie hesitated for a moment. 'I'm not prepared to come if you are worrying to marry me every minute.'

'Not at all, my dear, not at all. You come as my housekeeper, I am sure that a widowed master of the house and his housekeeper often sit together in the evenings. I would not be able to take you on social visits, but no matter, I am contented at home. And it would be good for Melia, too. She is not behaving herself very well at the moment.'

'How old is she, Uncle Jack?'

'She is eighteen and imagines herself to be in love with Frank Sherwood who is the coachman at the Hall. You remember Buckmoor Hall just up the dale from Pexton? Sir Ambrose French lives there with his daughter, Louisa.'

Lizzie nodded.' Yes, we used to ride our ponies in that direction.' She looked at him. He was nodding thoughtfully.

'Yes, Lizzie, fair enough. We will forget about the man and wife idea for the time being. You come as my housekeeper, that will suit me admirably, even if I do feel a little disappointed at your decision.

'Good, good, let us shake hands on it. We will go and tell them the good news and then make all the arrangements for your move to Glaisdale.'

★　★　★

Lizzie found that the days passed in a flash, and on the following Sunday, Mr and Mrs Flintoff sadly moved in with George and Cathy, and James Wilkes arrived in his trap to take Lizzie to Pexton House.

Her clothes were neatly packed in a small trunk and she carried a carpet bag with the things which were precious to her; some books, a china doll she had treasured since she was small, and most important of all, a parting gift from her mother and father.

Mr Flintoff had found a small sandalwood box and placed in it some of his favourite pieces of jet which included an intricate patterned locket which contained a small photograph of Mrs Flintoff.

They had to drive only a mile or two out of Whitby before turning down the lane which would lead to Egton Bridge and then on to Glaisdale End.

Lizzie felt gloomy and sad, but Mr Wilkes talked nicely to her and did not press on her his natural joviality. Miss Elizabeth Flintoff looked a fine young lady that day and he was carefully nursing his hopes of her becoming his wife soon.

Mr Wilkes was speaking quietly to her. 'Lizzie, I want to say something to you before we arrive at Pexton House, it is nothing very serious and I hope you will agree.'

She looked up at him. She had appreciated his forbearance on the journey and hoped that he was not going to spoil things by renewing his offer of marriage.

'I know that I have always been 'Uncle Jack' to you,' he said, 'but I think that your position as my house-keeper means that we must think of something more suitable.'

Lizzie smiled. 'Yes, of course, Uncle Jack, I do agree with you. I will remember to call you Mr Wilkes.'

But he was shaking his head. 'No, my dear, I consider that is far too formal. I would like you to call me James.'

She frowned. 'I am not sure that it is correct for a housekeeper,' she said slowly.

'Never mind what is correct. We have only ourselves to consider and I would prefer it to be James when we are on our own. You can refer to me as Mr Wilkes if you wish.'

Lizzie nodded, she did not want to start off her new position with a disagreement. 'Very well, it shall be James and I do hope that I will remember. I am sure that I will always think of you as Uncle Jack.'

'Louisa calls me James.'

'Louisa?' Lizzie questioned.

'Yes, Miss Louisa French. I think I told you that she lives with her father at Buckmoor Hall. They are our nearest neighbours and Louisa is a fine young woman. It is my wish that she will marry my son, Stephen, but he is not making it easy. You remember Stephen? He is not a lot older than you.'

'He lives at Pexton House?' she asked.

'No, he's in York. Quite the scholar at the Yorkshire Museum, not my style at all. I am afraid to say that we don't see eye to eye.'

I've discovered one thing, said Lizzie to herself. Mary and I thought there was a coolness between Uncle Jack and his eldest son; it looks as though I will not be meeting the Stephen who teased me all those years ago. She thought it sensible to change the subject.

A few minutes later they were driving along the narrow lane which wound its way up the dale to the hamlet of Glaisdale Head. In less than a mile, they were through wide gates and down the short drive to Pexton House. It was a rambling old building, but retained a certain graciousness. Its land ran down to Glaisdale Beck then rose on the opposite side to Egton High Moor.

But it was not the friendly and comfortable Mrs Hamlyn who awaited their arrival at the front door.

Standing in the porch was a very slim imperious-looking lady with fair hair piled high and stylishly dressed in a coat and skirt of dark green satin, the jacket close-fitting, the skirt full and elegantly pleated. The hat over the fairness of the hair was an elaborate confection of plumes and flowers which made her even taller.

She was not smiling and Lizzie thought she looked severe.

Then James spoke and there was a note of surprise in his voice. 'Goodness gracious, if it isn't Louisa. She must have thought it her duty to be here to welcome you. Let me help you down, my dear Lizzie.'

3

Lizzie felt dowdy beside Miss Louisa French as James introduced them. They stood in the entrance hall just inside the front door of Pexton House.

'Lizzie, I would like to introduce you to Miss Louisa French. She is our nearest neighbour at Buckmoor Hall where she lives with her father, Sir Ambrose. He's an old friend of mine, but I'm afraid that he does not enjoy the best of heath. Louisa, this is Miss Elizabeth Flintoff, who is to be my housekeeper.'

Lizzie thought she could hear scorn as well as superiority in the older woman's voice. 'You seem young to be a housekeeper, Miss Flintoff, I hope you know how to run a big house like Pexton.'

'I have been accustomed to helping my mother run our home in Whitby,' replied Lizzie with composure. She was not going to let Miss Louisa French know that 'home' had been one room behind a shop and two bedrooms. She did not count the attic which had been the boys' bedroom when they had been at home and disused for many years.

James Wilkes was regarding the pair of them. Louisa so straight and good-looking and haughty, while Lizzie was to him, comely and desirable. I think I had better keep the two of them apart, he chuckled to himself, I must remember that Lizzie is regarded only as a servant by Louisa. But there, he thought seriously, I have said that Louisa would make a good wife for Stephen, and I know that she is keen on the match. She is over thirty years of age and well and truly a spinster.

He addressed himself to Miss French. 'Come into the drawing-room, Louisa. Mrs Hamlyn will bring us tea and then she can show Lizzie around the house and take her to her room. Ah, here is Mrs Hamlyn now.'

A short, plump lady, beaming with a big smile, came hurrying from the direction of the kitchen. 'Miss Lizzie, I haven't forgotten you and I am very pleased that you are coming here as housekeeper.' She turned to Mr Wilkes. 'Would you like me to bring tea for you and Miss French, sir?'

Lizzie felt thankful for the friendliness of Mrs Hamlyn and followed her into the kitchen. A tray of tea was taken to the drawing-room by one of the maids and another pot was made for Mrs Hamlyn and Lizzie.

★　★　★

Mrs Hamlyn was remembering the old days, then between them they arranged Lizzie's duties. They would agree the meals between them, Lizzie would see to supplies being delivered from the village store, and once a week, Mrs Hamlyn would go to Whitby market.

Lizzie was left with the feeling that there was little for her to do, except when they had visitors. She was more than happy to arrange the dinner menus and she knew that it was her duty to give the orders to the calling tradesmen, and then to keep all the various accounts in order. There were three maids and she did not think that supervising their work and the care of the linen would cause her any difficulty.

Mrs Hamlyn seemed eager to have a chat. 'And if I might say so, Miss Lizzie — I can't bring myself to call you Miss Flintoff, though I know I should — I think it would be a kindness if you could sit with the Master in the evenings. I know it is not usually expected of a housekeeper, but he misses the company of the late Mrs Wilkes so much.

'After all, the Wilkes and the Flintoffs have always been as equals. It's only your sad misfortune that has brought you to the post of housekeeper. I will say no more, Miss Lizzie, for I know what was in the Master's mind for he talked to me in his loneliness. But what

I will say is that I think you made the right decision and I hope we will all settle down happy.'

Lizzie did settle down happily, but this was after an exchange of words with Miss French and happened on the very day of her arrival. She discovered later that Miss French was usually only to be seen at Pexton House when Stephen was paying them a visit.

That day, Miss French stayed to have dinner with Mr Wilkes, and Lizzie dined on her own in the sitting-room she had been given as housekeeper. She did appreciate having her own room, for she knew that she could sit quietly and do the accounts.

She was looking at the neat figures of the late Rhoda Wilkes when there came a tap on the door. Expecting it to be one of the maids, she got up to find out what was wanted.

To her surprise, she found Louisa French standing there.

'Miss French,' she said quietly. 'Do come in.'

The elegant woman swept into the room and sat herself in a chair by the fireplace.

Lizzie sat opposite the visitor but said nothing. She was puzzled by the visit.

'I have come to tell you, Miss Flintoff, that I am pleased for James' sake that he now has a housekeeper. I might disapprove of him choosing one so young, but that is by the way and I am sure that you will be most efficient. I understand that you have been helping to run your father's jet shop and I am sorry to hear that the business has failed. It is a worrying time for the jet craftsmen of Whitby.'

Lizzie was surprised at the sympathy in Miss French's sentiments. Perhaps I have misjudged her, she thought. 'It's a great pleasure to me to be here at Pexton House,' she said formally. 'I have fond childhood memories of my visits here.'

'That is precisely why I wish to speak to you.' The frost is back in her voice, thought Lizzie. 'I believe you knew

42

Stephen Wilkes before he went up to Oxford.'

Puzzled, Lizzie nodded and spoke quietly. 'Yes, it seems a long time ago. I've not seen him for many years.'

'He is an archaeologist and spends part of his time working here at Pexton House. For the rest of the time, he has a position at the Yorkshire Museum, he seems to be an authority on long barrows or some such thing. He has become quite scholarly.' She paused and Lizzie wondered where it was all leading.

'It is not my habit to call often at Pexton House, but I do come when Stephen is at home. We are betrothed and it is our only chance of meeting. Mr Wilkes is very keen on the match and this is what I wish to say to you. Are you listening?'

Lizzie stiffened. What was this dreadful woman going to say next? I must try and be patient if Uncle Jack thinks so highly of her, she told herself.

'There is nothing wrong with my

hearing, Miss French.' The words slipped out and Lizzie was appalled, she had meant to be so polite.

'There is no need for impertinence. I simply wish to know if I have your full attention.'

'Yes, certainly I am listening, Miss French.' Lizzie did not know how she kept her temper. She was not easily aroused but Louisa French was insolent and unbearably superior.

'I am glad to hear it for I wish you to know that I want no interference from you when Stephen is at home. No striking up a friendship because of old times. I am going to marry Stephen and I don't want his attentions diverted by his father's housekeeper. Stephen Wilkes is mine, do you hear?'

And with these incredible words, she got up and walked to the door and let herself out of the room.

Lizzie started to laugh. She is a female monster, she was thinking. How can Uncle Jack possibly want her for Stephen? But that performance was for me, was it not? She is a jealous woman and determined to be sure of acquiring Stephen Wilkes as a husband for herself. I wonder what Stephen's side of the story is? There is something that doesn't make sense. Miss Louisa French must be all of thirty-five and I know that Stephen is only twenty-seven. Is it any wonder that Mary and I thought that there was some mystery surrounding Stephen? I must try and find out.

Only half-an-hour after Miss French had left her, Lizzie had another visitor. There came a tap on the door and afterwards, Lizzie thought that there could not possibly have been a greater contrast between her two callers.

For Amelia Wilkes was eighteen years of age and looked younger, she could be described as petite, her corn-coloured hair shaped her head in loose curls not in the least fashionable, and she had blue eyes and a mischievous grin. Her name had always been shortened to Melia.

45

She came quickly up to Lizzie and kissed her cheek. 'I am so glad that you have come, Lizzie. Housekeeper sounds very grand, but I'm very sorry to learn about the shop. It'll be lovely to have you here, I miss Mama so much and I am afraid that Louisa does not approve of me. Have you met Louisa? She is Miss Louisa French of Buckmoor Hall, you remember we used to ride over as far as the hall on our ponies? That's how I met Frank.'

Lizzie sensed trouble in the way Melia had made this statement with such an air of defiance.

'Who is Frank?' she asked and waited.

The outburst of words from Melia did not surprise her. 'Oh, Lizzie. He is the most handsome young man you have ever seen. He is older than me. I'm eighteen and he's twenty-four, but it doesn't seem to matter. We love each other, Lizzie, but I am in such trouble. Mama liked Frank, she always said that it was love which was important and not your position in society. She was so understanding.

'You see she had been nursery maid to Stephen after his mother died. That was until he was sent away to school when he was eight years old — Papa thought that was best for him. So Mama was supposed to leave Pexton House, but she and Papa had fallen in love and they were married. Then I was born and then Jimmy. You won't have met Jimmy yet, he's staying with friends up the dale for a few days. Jimmy is only a year younger than me and he is a scamp, he really is. He chases the maids and I am sure he will fall in love with you, he is waiting to go to Oxford in the autumn.' Melia paused and grinned.

'I am talking a long time telling you all this, but you see, I have no-one to talk to, and I do want you to know about Frank. Papa won't agree to us being married. It is not that he doesn't like Frank, everybody likes Frank. He is Sir Ambrose French's coachman. Sir Ambrose is quite elderly and won't have anything to do with the railway, he calls them new-fangled, noisy and dirty. 'Give me a coach and horses any day,' he is fond of saying. So although he is a sick man — I believe he has consumption — he loves to ride out in his landau or his carriage.

'Sir Ambrose has given Frank a small cottage on the Buckmoor estate, so if we married, we would have somewhere to live. I wouldn't mind being a coachman's wife, Lizzie, I would feel honoured . . . ' Her voice tailed off.

'But your father will not agree to it?' asked Lizzie gently.

Melia shook her head violently. 'No, and I think he is most unreasonable. Just because he is the owner of Pexton House. He came from humble beginnings for I know that he was apprenticed to your father before he married Stephen's mother. He inherited Pexton Hall when she died, and her fortune, too.'

But Lizzie hesitated. 'I sympathise with you wanting to marry your Frank if you love him, Melia. But you are very young and I can understand your father not wishing for the match. I know I have always been your friend, but now I am just the housekeeper and I am bound to agree with Mr Wilkes.'

Melia grinned. 'He wanted to marry you! He told me that I was going to have a new mama. I was quite pleased when he told me that it was going to be you. But you must have refused him, Lizzie. Was it because you loved someone else?'

Lizzie shook her head. 'No, there was no-one else. But I always considered that I would only marry the man I loved. I am fond of your father, but he has always been 'Uncle Jack' to me, also he is so much older than I am. When I suggested that I came as housekeeper, he seemed quite pleased.'

'And here you are, and I know you will be my friend.'

'Do not expect me to encourage your marriage to Frank, Melia, if your father thinks it wrong, then I must feel the same.'

Melia was not daunted by this statement. 'Wait until you have met him,' she said brightly. 'I am sure that you will change your mind.'

They proceeded to chat about old times until Melia announced that she was going for a walk and she said it in such a way that Lizzie guessed that she was going to meet Frank.

It was not to be the last of the conversations on the day of Lizzie's arrival at Pexton House. No sooner than Melia had disappeared than James Wilkes came seeking Lizzie out.

'Lizzie,' he smiled as he stood in the doorway of her room. 'A whole day has passed and I have not spoken a word to you. I trust that you are comfortable. Come into the drawing-room, we will be cosy there and I want to hear about your day. I have been having dinner with Louisa, not an onerous task as she is very entertaining.'

Lizzie looked at him sharply to see if he was joking with her. She would hardly have described Louisa as 'entertaining'. But he was pleasantly serious and she followed him into the drawing-room.

She had only vague memories of this room, for as children, they had been out of doors or in the kitchen with Mrs Hamlyn. She found it to be a large and very handsome room, placed on the corner of the big house and with the main window facing across the dale and looking up to the moor. A smaller side window — carefully built to look right up the dale — afforded a splendid view and caught the morning sunshine.

Lizzie glanced around her. 'It is a lovely room, James — there I remembered — and you seem to be very fond of landscape paintings.' She could not help but notice that almost every inch of wall space was taken up with paintings.

'Yes, I like water colours and I go to sales all over the county seeking out the best Yorkshire scenes. Look, I even have one of the harbour at Whitby, I am fond of that one.'

Lizzie enjoyed picking out the places she knew on the large painting and then was invited to sit opposite Mr Wilkes across the large fireplace.

'This is very pleasant, my dear Lizzie, I trust that it will be the first of many such occasions. And sometimes, perhaps, you will join us for dinner. I am sure that Melia and Jimmy will benefit from your company. Jimmy is not here at the moment, but I have no doubt that Melia was anxious to renew her acquaintance with you.'

'Yes, I have seen both Melia and Miss French today, I have been quite busy.'

'I am glad for I am in quite a quandary to know what to do about Melia, she can be a little minx if she wishes to be. I am afraid that my dear Rhoda spoiled her. No doubt she told you about Frank Sherwood.'

'She did speak of a Frank, I did not hear his surname. You do not approve of the association?'

He frowned and shook his head. 'It will not do, Lizzie. One cannot find fault with Frank, he is an excellent coachman and a well-mannered young man. My good friend, Ambrose, thinks very highly of him. But Melia has been brought up the young lady and I have it in mind that she should marry young Welburn. He is a nephew of Sir Ambrose and their country house and estate are over at Lealholme. It would be an ideal arrangement for it would not take Melia too far from me.'

Lizzie wondered what Melia thought about it, she had spoken only of Frank. 'Melia is not agreeable?' was all she said.

'Won't hear of it. She thinks only of Frank Sherwood and it will not do. Can't have her marry a coachman. I hope that your presence here will make her see sense, Lizzie.'

'I doubt it,' Lizzie replied. 'I think perhaps she is rather headstrong, but I will see what I can do.'

'And what do you think of Miss

Louisa French? Is she not a fine young woman?'

This is going to be difficult, thought Lizzie. 'I hardly know her, but she is very striking. She came to tell me of her betrothal to Stephen. You are happy with it?'

'Happy?' He gave a loud laugh. 'I arranged it. They have grown up together and she fell in love with him. Couldn't be a better match for a son of mine. Poor Ambrose is not long for this world and Buckmoor House is willed to Louisa as there is no heir. Stephen will have a splendid home and he will be near, which will suit me. All we need now is to find me a nice little wife!'

'Uncle Jack.' The words slipped from Lizzie as a warning.

'No, I'm not going to say anything, dear girl. You have only just arrived and in any case, I want to see Stephen and Louisa settled.'

'Stephen is keen on the match?' she asked and was curious about the answer she would receive.

'No, Stephen is not keen. It is my opinion that Louisa presses him too much to settle a date for their marriage. But it will all come about, I am sure of that. And you can help me to persuade Stephen.'

Lizzie laughed. 'Stephen would not take any notice of me, James. I was always just a young whipper-snapper to him!' A thought occurred to her. 'But how old is Stephen now, he must be nearly thirty.'

'He is twenty-seven and time he settled down. I've no idea what he gets up to in York. Spends a lot of time at the museum when he isn't working at home. But why do you ask his age? You know very well that he is about five years older than you.'

She wondered if she dared to say her next words. 'But Miss French is a lot older than that, is she not?'

'Yes, of course she is. I believe she is thirty-five, but that need not make any difference. She is a fine young woman and will make Stephen a good wife.' He paused as he saw laughter come into her eyes. 'What is it, Lizzie? What is there to laugh at?'

Lizzie put a hand to her mouth. 'I'm sorry, Uncle Jack, but it suddenly came to me. Wouldn't Louisa be a better wife for you than she is for Stephen?'

His expression was incredulous. 'Louisa a wife for me? Whatever are you talking about? Of course she is the right age, no doubt about that and I would have Buckmoor Hall when Ambrose goes, there's something in what you say, I must admit. But the girl has been in love with Stephen for as long as I can remember, wouldn't look at me. No, Lizzie, I will get Stephen and Louisa together somehow and you will help me.'

She laughed again. 'I don't think that either Stephen or Miss French will take any notice of what I have to say. I will be honest and tell you that Louisa has already informed me that Stephen is her property.'

'Has she, by jove? It goes to show that she is determined to have him, so we will wait and see. Now we will have a little supper, Lizzie. Dinner is early here so I always have something light at supper time. But not in the dining-room. Mrs Hamlyn will send in some ham or tongue and we will eat by the fire. I am pleased that you are here even if you are my housekeeper and not my wife.'

★　★　★

The first week at Pexton House passed very quickly for Lizzie. She soon became accustomed to the smooth running of the house and did not find her duties onerous.

She saw no more of Louisa French, but Melia was an amusing companion and somewhat of a chatterbox. She persuaded her father to let Lizzie have a pony and to give his permission for them to ride out each afternoon. Lizzie protested that it was hardly in the duties of a housekeeper, but was easily over-ruled and she enjoyed her rides with Melia.

On her first weekend, she noticed that a gig had been driven round to the stables and that James had a visitor. She kept quiet in her room and did not have her usual ride as Melia was out visiting neighbours in the village.

Thinking that she would go and ask Mrs Hamlyn for some tea, she opened the door of her sitting-room at the same time as the drawing-room door was opened. She heard James' voice, but the gentleman who stepped into the hall at the same time as herself was not Mr Wilkes.

He was extremely tall and was dressed formally in jacket and trousers of matching grey worsted. His hair and eyes were as dark as her own and they stood staring at each other.

Lizzie had the feeling that she should know him, but started to turn away in embarrassment.

'Wait a moment,' came a commanding but pleasant voice.

She turned and their eyes met. 'Who . . . who are you?' she stammered, half-knowing what the answer was going to be.

'I'm Stephen, Lizzie.'

And Elizabeth Flintoff looked at the grown-up Stephen Wilkes and fell in love.

4

As Mr Stephen Wilkes walked towards her, Lizzie held her breath. Memories of the young Stephen came flooding back, the fun, the games, the laughing and that last chase in the wood when he had kissed her.

And here was the adult Stephen, with smiling dark eyes and his hands outstretched to greet her. She took a deep breath as he reached out and took both her hands in his. I can't suddenly fall in love with a grown-up Stephen, she told herself sternly, he is betrothed to Louisa and can never be for me.

His voice reached her as he held her hands. 'If it isn't my little Lizzie Flintoff, grown into a lovely young lady. Will you let me kiss you? I seem to remember another kiss, a stolen one.'

Lizzie could not keep the gladness from her voice and she laughed. 'I may have grown into a young lady, but I can never be described as lovely, Stephen. And I am Miss Flintoff, your father's housekeeper, now. I certainly cannot allow kisses. But it is very nice to meet you again . . . ah, here is your father.'

Mr Wilkes came out of the drawing-room and stood looking at the pair of them. 'So you have met again,' he said jovially. 'I am very pleased. Stephen, take Lizzie for a walk in the garden and remember old times. And, Lizzie, don't forget that I am relying on you to persuade Stephen in Louisa's favour.'

Stephen still had Lizzie's hand in his. 'Will you come, Lizzie? Shall we walk down to the beck, it is not too late in the evening. Do you need a shawl?'

Lizzie felt dazed. Her feelings were stunned by this meeting and by the overwhelming flood of emotion which was flowing through her.

'No, it is not cold, I would like to come.' It is dangerous, she told herself, but how can I say no?

At the back of Pexton House, the

land sloped downwards to Glaisdale Beck. At Stephen's side, Lizzie walked quietly over the lawn towards the vegetable garden and orchard. Neither of them spoke until they reached the beck, Lizzie did not know if the silence was awkwardness or a spell of enchantment at their meeting again.

The bubbling of the water over the stones broke the silence for them and it was Stephen who spoke first. 'Do you remember, Lizzie, that we put stepping stones so that we could go over the beck and up the hill to the wood on the other side?'

She nodded with a nice smile. 'Shall we see if we can find them? Though they might have been washed away in some of the storms we have had.'

They walked along the edge of the water and sure enough, in the exact place they had expected, they found the broad flat stones they had placed in the water all that time ago.

'It's just the same and the water is low so the stones are quite dry.' Lizzie looked at him and was surprised at the solemn expression on his face. 'Why do you look so solemn, Stephen?' she asked him.

He shook his head. 'I'm not sure. The happiness of those days had come back to me, we can remember them but they are gone for ever. You can never recapture your youth, Lizzie.'

'We can try,' she said light-heartedly.

'Whatever do you mean?' he asked.

'Let's just cross the beck just as we used to and see what happens.'

'Lizzie Flintoff, we are grown up now, both of us in our twenties. We should have put away childish things.'

Lizzie laughed. 'I dare you to cross the beck first and then to help me over.' She could feel an imp of mischief in her, something new to her after these last weeks of worry.

Stephen laughed, too, and suddenly looked younger. 'I cannot resist a dare, can I? Here I go.'

And she watched him balance him-self carefully on the stones before jumping on to the opposite bank. 'Now your turn,' he called to her. 'I'll catch you.'

'Here I come,' she called back, and lifted her long skirt to stop it trailing in the water.

All went well until she reached the last stone when she accidentally caught her foot in the hem of her dress and fell forward. Not into the water, but into Stephen's waiting arms.

He clutched her to him and she looked up, laughing. She saw his smiling eyes as he bent his head to find her lips. The kiss took her breath away and she let it continue with a sudden longing to be able to stay in his arms for ever.

As he raised his head and looked at her, she could only whisper. 'What happened?'

'I kissed you. I wanted to kiss you and I am glad I did. Are you glad, Lizzie?' he asked the question quietly.

But with her feet now on firm ground, common sense was returning to Lizzie. 'Of course I am not glad! You shouldn't have done it, we aren't children any more and you should be thinking of Louisa.'

'Forget Louisa!' His words were explosive.

'Stephen,' Lizzie said in horror. 'You should not speak like that. Your father told me that you are going to marry Louisa and I am sure that Louisa is in love with you.'

'Lizzie, I have no doubt that my father has asked you to try and persuade me in Louisa's favour. He knows that I'm hesitating, although I realise that it would be a good match for me. I've known Louisa all my life and she is a fine young woman. If I married her, Buckmoor Hall would be mine one day and that would suit me very nicely.'

Lizzie looked puzzled. 'Why do you say that?'

'You do not know the grown up Stephen very well, Lizzie, not yet. I'm an archaeologist and it is my ambition to write a book on the archaeology of the North Riding of Yorkshire. Already I'm doing some work on the subject when I'm at Pexton House, but I need my position at the Yorkshire Museum to finance me.

'I'm out and about everywhere examining the finds on archaeological sites which are being excavated, and it's an expensive business. Another factor is that I find the city stifling. I grew up here and I miss the dale very much when I'm in York.' He paused thoughtfully then continued in a more positive way.

'Father would provide me with an income, but I don't wish for that. Neither do I think it would be successful if I was at Pexton House all the time. Do you understand, Lizzie? I'm taking a long time to explain all these things to you.'

She nodded. 'If Sir Ambrose dies and your married Louisa, you would have no financial problems and you could work at Buckmoor Hall. It makes sense,

Stephen, why did you hesitate?'

'I don't love Louisa.' It was a bald statement and came as a shock to Lizzie. What should she say to him?

Her reply came slowly. 'Is that important to you?'

He did not answer her immediately. They were standing, the two of them, at the edge of the beck, not looking at each other but staring at the endless fascination of clear, sparkling water running swiftly over the stones.

'I can tell you, Lizzie, I don't know why. We only met again five minutes ago! I don't love Louisa, I suppose I am fond of her in a strange kind of way and we are comfortable together. But is it enough? That's what I keep asking myself. I feel that when I marry, it would have to be to someone I loved very much, fondness is not enough in my opinion.'

Lizzie gave a quick intake of breath and Stephen heard it. 'What is it, Lizzie, what have I said?'

She turned to him. The longer she

was with him, the closer the old Stephen became. She gave a little grin. 'You used almost the same words that I said to myself when I knew I couldn't marry Uncle Jack . . . '

'Marry my father? Never. I can't believe he asked you, he must be twice your age and it would make you my step-mother. I never heard anything so ridiculous.' He took her hands. 'Tell me it is not true, Lizzie.'

She laughed and let her hands lie in his, she liked his hold. 'It is quite true, and I refused and suggested I came as housekeeper instead. And here I am, though I think he still hopes that I will change my mind. Did he not tell you abut it?'

Stephen shook his head. 'No, we haven't been getting on very well since I refused to let him finance me and then wouldn't consider Louise as a wife. But I've let him think that I still have it in mind, for I can see the sense of having a rich wife and living at Buckmoor Hall. It would make my work so much easier.

I keep wishing that something would happen to make me decide one way or another. I know that is feeble of me, do you think it feeble, Lizzie?'

She replied softly. 'Stephen, I think most gentleman would have jumped at the chance of a rich, good-looking wife like Louisa, but you have put love first. I consider that to be honest and I admire you for it.'

'You admire me, Lizzie?'

She smiled. 'I don't know yet! I used to think you were a pest, but they were happy times. We didn't have the cares we have now we are older. But you must not forget that your father is relying on me to push you into Louisa's arms.'

He gave a mock sigh. 'Oh dear, I think I've heard enough on the subject of Louisa for the moment. Perhaps by the end of the week, I will have made up my mind about her, though having you here is not going to help matters.'

'Whatever do you mean by that?' asked Lizzie.

'Never mind, it is getting cold and I will help you over the stepping stones and we will return to Pexton House and have some supper with Father. But we won't tell him about the kiss!'

'No, Stephen, we will not,' said Lizzie.

★   ★   ★

Before the end of Stephen's week at home, fate had taken a hand in his affairs, for Sir Ambrose French died and was laid to rest.

The circumstance caused many changes for them all. Stephen did not return to York when he had intended to, but waited until after the funeral. The young James Wilkes — or Jimmy as he was affectionately known by his family — returned from the protracted visit to his friends. Louisa was at Pexton House every day, dressed all in black and managing to look very fashionable. She was not visibly upset at her father's death for it had been long expected, though she did have a lot to say to Stephen on the subject. He had been working quietly in the library when she was shown in on the day after the funeral.

'Stephen, I wish to talk to you before your return to York. I believe that we can make our plans now, though of course any wedding ceremony will have to be delayed until I am out of mourning.'

Stephen looked closely at the woman who was planning to marry him almost without even beginning to consider his wishes or inclinations. Her father and his father had been eager for the match and that was enough for Louisa. There is no softness in her expression at all, Stephen thought, and somehow Lizzie's ready smile came into his mind.

Louisa is calculating and determined to have things her own way, he thought, but I must listen to what she has to say, my future depends on it.

Louisa continued as though she could not wait for his reply. 'I have always cared for you, Stephen, and have waited for this moment for a long time. The will has been read, and as I thought, I am the sole heir and will be the owner of Buckmoor Hall as soon as the legal formalities have been completed. I have no wish to be living at the hall on my own and I would like to be married as soon as the conventions allow it.

'Of course, I will wear black for the year required for the death of a father, but I knew that dear Papa would have wished us to be married as soon as possible. He did not want me to be left on my own, and I think that we can respectfully arrange our marriage for six months time.' She paused, but did not give him a chance to speak.

'What are your thoughts on the matter, Stephen? I do want you to know that I honour your professional ambitions and appreciate that there will be times when you wish to be away examining your archaeological sites. You will have every opportunity to pursue your profession at Buckmoor Hall and with no financial worry. I will be a wealthy person and all that is mine will be yours.'

Stephen had listened to this lengthy speech with a deepening sense of gloom. All that Louisa had said was true and had been said with a genuine generosity, he would be free to roam the whole of the North Riding and to write up his finds afterwards. He would not be tied to a job he disliked, he would be back in Glaisdale. He should be overjoyed at such an opportunity, but he knew that any feelings of joy were far distant.

And he remembered his reply to Lizzie. 'I do not love her'. Did love matter when everything else was so right? Should he put love before his ambition, his career? Did his regard, rather than his love for Louisa stand in the way of this splendid opportunity?

Louise brought him back to her attention. 'You are taking a very long time to reply, Stephen,' she said and he thought her tone was shrewish. Then it was as though she had regretted her remark for she suddenly smiled and put out a hand to him.

It was the first time she had made any such gesture and he took her hand in his without thinking. It somehow surprised him that her fingers were soft and warm, and her smile had made her seem less distant. He tried to excuse her former stiffness with him, telling himself that perhaps her father's long illness had worried her.

Was there a hope that he could make this marriage work? He still doubted it, but he made up his mind not to dismiss her entirely while she was still grieving for her father.

And then it happened, that as he made his reply, Stephen realised that although it was Louisa's hand he was holding, it was Lizzie he was seeing in his mind's eye. A touch, a smile, a kiss and Lizzie Flintoff was in front of him. I must be mad, he thought, about to consider marrying Louisa when Lizzie has suddenly come back into my life.

Then he chided himself. Don't be a fool, think of the advantages of marrying Louisa, think of the wonderful opportunity for fulfilling his ambitions.

So the words came, pleasant but guarded. 'Louisa, we have known each other for so long and there is a lot of respect between us. I am fully aware that you cannot marry until your period of mourning is over, so I would suggest that we continue as the good friends we have always been. Then at the end of that time, we can consider our betrothal.'

Louisa felt she had won her battle for Stephen's affections and smiled at him. 'Thank you, Stephen, you are very understanding as I thought you would be. Your father will be pleased.'

She stood up and prepared to leave. Stephen thought that she looked tall and dignified and he never knew what prompted his next words.

'May I kiss you, Louisa?' he asked her.

A flush came into Louisa's face, a deep red of annoyance and embarrassment. 'Stephen, I am shocked. How dare you suggest such a thing? We are not even betrothed. Please remember that I am a woman of property and fortune, not one of your maids or the housekeeper. I do not expect such behaviour from you and I will leave you.'

Silently, a wooden-faced Stephen opened the door for her. As soon as she had left the room, he sat back in his chair and laughed. He laughed out loud, heartily. Be damned to it, he was thinking, I cannot marry a statue like that and I suppose I should have seen her off. But I didn't and now I must ask if I have committed myself to a betrothal? I hope not.

Anything can happen in six months. Miss Louisa French might be a woman of property, and her fortune might aid my career, but I'm deuced if I wouldn't be happier with Lizzie even if it meant continuing to live and work in York. Come to think of it, I haven't seen Lizzie for a couple of days, I'll go and find her now.

During the days which Stephen had just referred to, when he had been busy at work in the library, Lizzie had managed to put behind her the episode by the beck. She was aware that Louisa was in the house every day, but she knew of the strict etiquette of mourning, and guessed that there would be no announcement of a betrothal.

Then Jimmy arrived home for Sir Ambrose's funeral, and it was as though a whirlwind had struck the house.

Although Lizzie had visited Pexton House in recent months, Jimmy had always been away at his school and it came as a shock to her when she met him again to find that he had grown into a handsome and flirtatious young gentleman.

It was Melia who told her of his arrival.

Melia had been rather subdued for a few days, and Lizzie wondered if there had been a lovers' tiff, for the young girl had been home in the evenings.

But that morning, Melia had arrived

in the housekeeper's sitting-room in good spirits and full of news. 'Lizzie, Jimmy is home, Papa sent for him to come in time for the funeral tomorrow. He is with Papa at the moment, but he is looking forward to meeting you again.'

Half-an-hour later, they all met up in the conservatory which Mr Wilkes had added at the back of the house. Tropical plants and ferns were in fashion and had been planted in stone urns, the chairs and tables were of wrought iron.

Lizzie walked out of the French windows into the warm glass-house to find Melia and Jimmy seated at a table talking earnestly to each other.

Jimmy, with a head of thick fair hair not unlike his sister's, jumped up. 'It's Lizzie Flintoff.' He rushed forward, took her hands and kissed her cheek at the same time. 'And all in grey just as a housekeeper should be, you look lovely, Lizzie. Are you pleased to see me?'

Lizzie laughed and sat down at the table with them. 'You haven't changed,

Jimmy, except to get taller and more handsome. Yes, I am pleased to see you. I hope you will cheer Melia up, she has been very quiet this week, but then it has been an upsetting time.'

'I didn't think that you have noticed, Lizzie,' Melia said. Her eyes were red and it appeared that she had been crying.

Jimmy laid his hand on top of his sister's, but he was looking at Lizzie. 'She took one look at me and burst into tears, but I soon discovered what was wrong. She and Frank have had a quarrel. I am going to help them.'

Lizzie felt alarmed. 'Melia knows very well that your father would never approve of a marriage between Sir Ambrose's — I suppose I should say the late Sir Ambrose's — coachman. I'm sure that Frank is an admirable young man, but I believe that Mr Wilkes wishes for a marriage for Melia with the Welburn family over at Lealholme.'

'Never,' Melia cried out. 'I want to marry the man I love, not a gentleman picked for me by my father.'

Oh dear, thought Lizzie, it is worse than I thought. 'You are very young Melia, you will think differently in a year or two.'

'No, I won't. It is Frank I love and I told him that we should run away to be married, but he has refused. He says it would be a disgrace, and that he will always be my friend and that I can always go to him if I am in trouble.'

It sounds as though he is a sensible young man, thought Lizzie, but I must say the right thing to Melia. 'Be guided by your father, Melia. He is a good man and only wants the best for you.'

Lizzie went about her duties, and the funeral over, she expected Stephen to return to York. But Louisa still continued to visit and she admired Stephen for the support he gave to his supposedly future wife at her time of trouble.

Melia cheered up and the afternoon pony rides resumed with Jimmy accompanying them on a fine Hunter. But

Lizzie was troubled by Jimmy's presence in the house. She found him to be an engaging young man and she did not dislike him. But she did dislike his absurd protestations of love and his snatching at her hand or waist at any opportunity.

On the day after the funeral, she had walked down to the herb garden to see if there was any fennel which Mrs Hamlyn needed for a recipe that day.

Lizzie did not know that Jimmy had followed her from the house and was catching up with her as she walked across the lawn to the vegetables and herbs.

'Lizzie,' he called.

She turned round quickly and saw him, he was dressed for riding and looked dashing. 'Jimmy, you are always creeping up on me when I least expect it. What is it this time?'

He gave a brilliant smile. 'Don't be cross with me, darling Lizzie, you know how much I love you.'

'Nonsense,' she retorted shortly and

81

turned again to proceed across the lawn.

'I want to ask you if you will come riding with me,' he said.

'Of course I cannot come riding with so many things to do in the mornings. I am on my way to look for fennel for Mrs Hamlyn.

He walked alongside her and took her arm. 'Then if I can't have a ride with you, I will take a kiss.'

'You will do nothing of the kind . . . let me go.'

But pull as she might, she could not stop him from bending down and claiming her lips. She struggled, and afterwards was never quite sure what happened next.

One minute, Jimmy was kissing her, the next he was lying flat on the grass with a shouting and cursing Stephen bending over him. For Stephen had come in search of Lizzie after his conversation with Louisa and had walked across the lawn and witnessed the scene between Jimmy and Lizzie.

Afterwards, and to his astonishment, he realised that his feelings were of jealousy, then found that jealousy gave place to rage.

He hit out at his half-brother and let Jimmy have the benefit of his anger. 'How dare you pester Lizzie with your attentions, Jimmy. Get up quickly, apologise and be on your way.'

5

Lizzie stared at the scene in front of her with horror. Jimmy was rising awkwardly from his fall and Stephen stood over him with a glare of anger. She found herself without words to describe her feelings. She did not speak until she saw Jimmy hurrying over the lawn towards the house having muttered a gruff 'Sorry, Lizzie' to her.

It was then she turned to Stephen and hot words escaped from her without her being able to prevent them.

'You must know that Jimmy is no more than a schoolboy and you know very well that you behaved in just the same way when you were his age. Do you think I am not able to handle the likes of your brother at the age of seventeen? It seems to be that the two of you are quick to snatch at kisses whenever you have the chance. Have you succeeded in kissing Louisa yet?'

She watched the angry expression in his face and could not believe that she had spoken to him in such a way. He glared at her.

'You will apologise for knocking Jimmy down. You behaved as though you were jealous that he had kissed me when all this week you have been closeted with the wealthy Miss French. Were you coming to tell me that your betrothal is to be announced?'

'I was coming to tell you, Miss Flintoff, that there is to be no talk of marriage between Louisa and myself while she is in mourning for her father. I think I will be better off with a dignified woman like Louisa who refuses any offer of a kiss — very properly, too — than with a shrew of a housekeeper called Lizzie Flintoff.'

'You are insulting, sir!'

'I meant to be.'

'Then you can stay and insult the herbs for I am going to pick the fennel for Mrs Hamlyn and I hope I do not have occasion to see you again before you return to York.'

Tears streamed down her face and she knew that she was crying not because she had been so rude to Stephen, but because she loved him.

She felt miserable for the rest of the day and knew that she should apologise to Stephen for her rudeness. But she did not see him again and thought that he had gone over to Buckmoor Hall. She did seem very contrite to Jimmy who promised to behave more properly towards her and swore vengeance on his older brother.

'I will kiss Louisa,' he announced as he left her and Lizzie laughed for the first time that day.

She made up her mind that she must try and see Stephen before he left for York, but although she rose early the next day and was about her duties in good time, she discovered that he had risen at dawn and had driven his trap to York without even stopping for breakfast.

There followed a strange two weeks. Jimmy was on his best behaviour. Melia went about happily enough and Lizzie guessed that she had made up her quarrel with Frank, and, oddly enough, Mr Wilkes was often to be found at Buckmoor Hall. In his kindly way, Lizzie imagined that he was supporting Louisa in her grief. Stephen was to be seen no more at Pexton House.

The peaceful days came to an abrupt end with the sudden disappearance of Melia. Although the young girl had seemed contented, Lizzie knew that soon after Sir Ambrose's funeral, Melia had quarrelled with her father once again over her intention of marrying the Buckmoor Hall coachman.

James Wilkes and Lizzie were progressing well together. To her relief, he made no more mention of marriage and he seemed glad to talk to her about his younger offspring. Of Stephen, he said little.

And so it happened, on a busy Friday, that Lizzie did not miss Melia until it was time for lunch. A meal that was always taken in the dining-room where Mr Wilkes had persuaded Lizzie to join him with Melia and Jimmy each day. That week, Jimmy had gone off again to stay with friends and James and Lizzie sat at the dining-table waiting for Melia to join them.

She did not appear and James was frowning. He liked punctuality.

'What has Melia been up to this morning, Lizzie?' he asked. 'Have you seen her?'

Lizzie shook her head. 'No, but I don't often see her in the mornings. She's late at breakfast, then sometimes she'll ride out. I've been busy with the bed linen all morning and I have hardly given her a thought.' She noticed the deep crease on his forehead. 'Do not worry yourself about her, James. She can't have come to any harm.'

'I'm thinking about Frank Sherwood.'

'Frank? No, no, I am sure that all is well with them. They did have a quarrel because she was trying to rush him into marriage. He refused, quite sensibly and I believe they have been going for walks on fine evenings, there is no more to it than that.'

'I wish I could think so,' he muttered. 'She still has not come and I refuse to start lunch without her. Just go upstairs and see if she is in her room, Lizzie, she may have forgotten the time, though she knows what I am like about sitting down to meals punctually.'

Lizzie did as she was told and hurried up the stairs to Melia's bedroom. The room was empty. Lizzie looked around her and had strange misgivings. It seemed oddly tidy, for Melia was an untidy miss, leaving it to the maids to clear up after her.

It was when Lizzie noticed that the brush, comb and mirror set were missing from the dressing-table that she had a sudden fear. The set was of silver and the backs of the hand-mirror and brush were patterned very prettily with small cherubs. The set had belonged to

Melia's mother and Lizzie knew that the girl treasured it.

I'll go and ask one of the maids, thought Lizzie, perhaps the brush and mirror are being polished. But it was a hope full of doubts, for any job such as that would have been done earlier in the morning.

She turned to go downstairs and as she did so, her eye was caught by the counterpane on the bed. There was nothing odd about the counterpane itself, but Melia had always kept a very favourite doll which sat on the pillow. It had a soft body and a pretty dress, but the head was of bisque porcelain and the hair was real and golden like Melia's. The doll was missing.

Lizzie stared and stared. In the place where the doll always sat was a square white envelope; the large letters printed on it said 'PAPA'.

Nervously, Lizzie picked it up. What in the world had Melia done?

Envelope in hand, she rushed down the stairs to the dining-room.

'Uncle Jack,' she cried out, using the old name in her anxiety. 'Melia is not there, but she has left a letter for you.'

James Wilkes rose from the dining-table and went forward, his hand outstretched. The letter was snatched from Lizzie's hand and furiously torn open.

'My God . . . ' he gasped as he read the words. He went white. His hand went to his chest and he sat down heavily on a chair.

'What is it? What has she done?'

'Read it,' he said, his voice was hoarse.

Lizzie took the letter from his hand and read the dreadful words.

Dear Papa,

By the time you receive this, I hope to be married to Frank. We have a nice house so please don't worry about me. Frank is going to write to you.

With love from Amelia.

For long moments, Lizzie did not know what to do. She looked first at the words with disbelief and then at the ashen face of James Wilkes.

He was still clutching at his chest, but managed to speak. 'Lizzie, we may be too late to stop her. Do what I tell you . . . send one of the stable boys in the trap for Dr Catchpole to come to me . . . then tell one of the maids to fetch Louisa . . . and, Lizzie, you go with the stable boy to Glaisdale End and get the train to York. You are to go to the Yorkshire Museum and find Stephen and bring him home. He must come and search for the silly girl, we may be in time.' He was in obvious pain and Lizzie did not like to leave him.

'I am not going to leave you until Louisa comes, James . . . you must lie down. Let me help you into the drawing-room and you can lie on the sofa. You are not to move and I am not going to give you brandy for it might make you worse . . . there you are, lie down and I will loosen your tie and undo your collar stud . . . now stay there while I send for Louisa.'

But Lizzie did not go in search of a maid, deciding that it would be quicker for her to ride the pony over to Buckmoor Hall. It would take much longer for a maid to go on foot.

The pony was saddled in seconds, and gathering up her full housekeeper's skirt, she was helped into the side-saddle by the stable boy. She went as fast as the pony could manage and was riding up the drive of Buckmoor Hall in seconds.

In all her weeks in Glaisdale, she had never been into the Hall, though she and Melia had often passed nearby.

A maid answered her loud knock and Louisa was with her in minutes.

'Whatever is it, Lizzie? What brings you here? Is Mr Wilkes all right?'

'No, he is not all right, Miss French. We have had bad news and it has brought about an attack of palpitations of the heart. I have left him lying down quietly, but please do you think you could come?'

'Yes, yes, of course. I'll come if James is ill, but what has happened to cause it?' Louisa sounded anxious.

'It's Melia,' Lizzie said hastily. 'She has disappeared and left a note for her father to say that she has run off and is going to marry Frank Sherwood . . . oh, please come.'

'But, Lizzie it is not possible. I dismissed Frank over two weeks ago, I did not need the carriage any longer. I always travel on the railway and I drive my own trap, as you know.'

Lizzie listened in disbelief. 'You mean that Frank has not been here?'

'No, I gave him a good reference and he left the next day. He seemed quite eager to be gone.'

Lizzie shook her head. 'It makes no sense at all. Please will you come and tell Mr Wilkes, he seemed most anxious to see you. And he wants me to go to York and ask Stephen to come home.'

Louisa nodded. 'Yes, you go ahead

and I'll get the trap and be with you in minutes. It is a good idea to fetch Stephen. We will need him here, though I'm sure I don't know what we are going to do.'

Louisa in her trap, and Lizzie on her pony arrived at Pexton House at the same time.

In the drawing-room Mr Wilkes held out his hand to Louisa. 'My dear girl, I knew you would come. I am sending for Dr Catchpole and Lizzie is going on the railway to York. She has told you what has happened? The shock of it has affected my heart and Lizzie says I must lie still. She is going to fetch Stephen and I will be so glad to have you stay with me.'

Lizzie was at the door. 'I will go now, Mr Wilkes, I couldn't have left you on your own. But I have no idea what time we will be back, possibly late this evening.'

'Be sure to bring Stephen home with you and he can go and hunt for Melia tomorrow . . . ' he paused for breath and held out Melia's letter. 'You had better take this with you, but we will let Louisa glance at it first.'

Lizzie took with her no more than a shawl in case it was evening when they returned, and a bag for her money. At Glaisdale Station, she had to wait more than an hour for the train which would take her to York. The journey seemed endless and she had to make a change to the Scarborough-York line. She eventually reached York Station at nearly five o'clock and knew that she would have to rush to find Stephen still at the museum.

She hurried down the hill from the station and almost ran through the gardens of the ruined St Mary's Abbey where the Yorkshire Museum was situated. It was a dignified, classical building erected in 1830. It housed many of the finest treasures of Yorkshire's history.

Lizzie was nervous as she climbed the steps, she could see a doorman standing at the entrance.

'Mr Wilkes?' he said when she asked for Stephen. 'And might I ask who wishes to see him?'

'Miss Flintoff,' Lizzie replied. 'And please tell him that it is urgent.'

Lizzie knew that she must look a poor picture. She had not had the time to put on a hat and her hair had got blown on the short trip to Glaisdale Station in the trap. She was still in her housekeeper's uniform and with her shawl round her shoulders, felt no more than a servant. Which is what I am, she thought ruefully, as she waited to see if Stephen had left the museum or not.

When he did appear, he was not looking in the best of tempers. 'Lizzie, how dare you come to the museum seeking me out. Are you in some sort of trouble? You look flustered.'

Aware that the museum attendant was still standing there and thinking that Stephen would not want his business known, she stood still and straight and spoke as formally as she could.

'Mr Wilkes, your father has sent me to find you on a very urgent family matter. I would be glad if I could talk to you privately.'

He seemed to sense that her manner was serious and gave a nod. 'I am about to leave the museum for my house. Give me time to lock up my room and I'll be with you.'

Lizzie walked down the steps and waited quietly. It was no more than five minutes before he joined her.

'We will walk in the abbey gardens,' he said and his voice was still tense. 'I imagine it must be a serious matter if Father has sent you all this way to find me. Did you come on the railway? Is my father ill?'

'We have had an upset and the shock of it brought on an attack of palpitations. Your father is lying down quietly awaiting Dr Catchpole.'

'Well, get on with it, whatever can have happened?'

'Melia has gone off with Frank Sherwood, I've brought the letter which she left for Mr Wilkes.'

Stephen stopped and faced her. 'You're not serious, Lizzie, give me the letter.' He took it from her and read it with growing anger. 'The stupid girl, the stupid little girl. Do you know where she has gone? Will we be in time to stop her or is it best to let her marry her love's young dream? God knows it is bad enough to have to marry when one's heart is not engaged.'

Lizzie thought the words strange and guessed he must be referring to Louisa. He seemed very disturbed and not just on Melia's account.

'What shall we do, Stephen?' she asked quietly.

'Sit down on this stone and let me think,' he said absentmindedly.

They were walking through the ruins of the old abbey and there were many low stones which made a good place to sit.

'Is my father on his own?' he asked next.

'No, he sent me for Louisa. She promised to stay with him.'

'Thank God, perhaps some good might come of it all,' he muttered.

Lizzie could not keep her thoughts to herself. 'Stephen, you are in an odd mood, has anything happened apart from Melia going off like that?'

He turned to her. 'Dear Lizzie, trust you to notice. And I think I owe you an apology for the last time we met . . . '

'No, no,' she interrupted quickly. 'I was very rude to you. I came to apologise the next morning but you had already left for York.'

He took her hands in his. 'We will forget it, and I will tell you what has happened today and then we will make some plans to go after Melia. It will have to be first thing tomorrow morning. At the museum this afternoon, I was offered a senior post. It is a great honour at my age, but it would upset all the plans I have made for myself. It means one of two things if I want to proceed with my research and my book. You know what those two things are?'

Lizzie could guess and she did not lack honesty or courage. 'You must settle in York and forget about your work on the archaeology of the North Riding, or you must marry Louisa and then you will have no financial problems and will be able to work on your book from Buckmoor House.'

He squeezed her hands. 'You understand me well enough, Lizzie, to know that I do not relish either option. But we must forget about my problems and concentrate on Melia. Do we know where she and Frank are?'

She shook her head. 'We have no idea unless Louisa knows where Frank went when he left Buckmoor Hall.'

'Frank has left Buckmoor Hall?'

Lizzie told him what Louisa had said and he frowned. 'So the first thing to do is to ask Louisa. Now for this evening's plans. Listen carefully. My house is just off Bootham and only a few minutes walk through the abbey; I rent the house and have a woman who comes in to clean for me and prepare my meals.

My trap and my horse are there. So I suggest that we hurry back there now, Mrs Gee will have a supper ready and there will be plenty for you. Then we can set off for Glaisdale before six o'clock. That will get us to Pexton House before dark.'

At Pexton House, Dr Catchpole had pronounced that James Wilkes was in no danger. He must rest for a day or two, eating only light meals, and to take no wine or brandy.

After he had gone, James and Louisa had dinner together. James did obey doctor's orders and ate very little.

The meal over, they settled in the drawing-room again. It was a cool evening and the logs blazed cheerfully in the big fireplace. James did not lie down again, but sat quietly chatting to Louisa.

'If I was not in such a worry over Melia,' he told Louisa, 'I would think of this as being very pleasant. We must do it more often when all this trouble is over. I'm going to try and put it from my mind and concentrate on the pleasure of your company, my dear.'

Louisa beamed with a sudden pleasure and happiness. Compliments did not often come her way. Certainly not from Stephen.

'When I do come over to Pexton House,' she told him, 'it's usually to see Stephen. But don't forget, James, that I have known you for many years, and Rhoda was my dearest friend. I miss her almost as much as you do.'

James Wilkes was looking at Miss Louisa French and seemed to be seeing her with new eyes. The friend of his wife? Good looking and wealthy? And now mistress of Buckmoor Hall? Why was he urging his son to marry her when she would make a good wife for himself? Forget about Lizzie Flintoff, he told himself, a good girl, but really too young for him. When all this fuss with Melia was over, he would try and discover if Louisa really did love Stephen as much as she said she did.

He gave an inward smile and felt

better. Stephen would find Melia and bring her back home again. Now he, James Wilkes, could enjoy an evening in Louisa's charming company.

'Would you like a game of backgammon, Louisa?' he asked her.

She glanced at him; he was certainly looking more like his usual self. 'Do you think you should, James?' she asked solicitously.

'Yes, I do,' he replied and got up to fetch the backgammon box.

For Stephen and Lizzie, it had been a quiet and swift journey back to Glaisdale. Stephen took the quiet back lanes from York to Kirbymoorside and from there, it was over the moor.

They arrived at Pexton House soon after nine o'clock and were surprised to find Mr Wilkes and Louisa engrossed in a game of backgammon.

'Father.' Stephen made a cheerful greeting. 'Have you recovered from your shock? Evening, Louisa it was kind of you to stay with Father.'

'She has been very patient with me,'

declared Mr Wilkes. 'And I stopped worrying about Melia, knowing that you were on your way.' He turned to Lizzie. 'Thank you very much for your efforts, Lizzie.'

The backgammon board was abandoned and tea was brought in.

Stephen began to question Louisa. 'Tell me, Louisa, I understand from Lizzie that you had to dismiss Frank Sherwood soon after Sir Ambrose died. How did Frank react? Did he tell you what he was going to do? And do you know if he has another place?'

Louisa didn't seem to object to the questions, and answered them carefully. 'Frank knew all along that I would not keep the carriage after Papa died, so I think he was quite prepared. I had the impression that he had already made his plans.'

She looked from one to the other. 'He has been an excellent coachman, you know, and I gave him six months wages. That was on top of the sum which Father had left him in the will.

Father thought the world of Frank and I must admit that a more pleasant or hard-working young man, you could not wish to meet.

'I know that you are upset at Melia running off with him and I can understand that, but she's so young. It puzzles me a little that Frank agreed to run off with her, it is not the kind of thing I would have expected of him.'

'Did he tell you what he was going to do?' repeated Stephen.

She shook her head. 'I had the feeling that he was not quite certain, as though he had something in mind, but it was not settled. He did say something about his parents so I imagined that he must have been going home to them.'

Stephen nodded. 'That sounds promising. Do you know where his home is?'

'Yes, his father is a respected and quite wealthy farmer over near Egton Bridge. It is very upsetting for you all, but I think you would do best to start off by speaking to Frank's parents.'

Stephen agreed. 'Thank you, Louisa, that is most helpful. I will accompany you back to Buckmoor Hall, it is getting dark.'

6

It was no more than three or four miles from Pexton House to Egton Bridge, and the following morning, Stephen and Lizzie set off in the trap soon after breakfast. To Lizzie's relief, it was a warm and dry morning. She left off her grey dress and wore a rust-coloured print of ribbed cotton, tight to the waist and with a gored skirt. The sleeves were full and long as had been the fashion for many years. With it, she wore a cream velvet bonnet perched on the back of her head and tied with brown ribbons under her chin.

Stephen was quick to compliment her as soon as she had settled in the trap. 'You look charming, Lizzie, the colour becomes you.'

She smiled. 'I am pleased to dispense with my grey for once!'

They talked very little as they drove

through the narrow lanes and once in Egton Bridge, Stephen called at the Wheatsheaf Inn to ask the whereabouts of the Sherwoods' farm. They were directed towards Grosmont and found Prospect Farm easily. The stone-built farmhouse was old and substantial, and the approach to it gave the impression of prosperity.

A maid answered Stephen's knock and they were shown into a low-ceilinged parlour where they were joined by a pleasant-looking woman dressed handsomely in dark green. She looked puzzled.

'You are enquiring after Frank?' she said.

Stephen introduced them as calmly as he could. 'I am the brother of Miss Amelia Wilkes. She is acquainted with your son, Frank, and we have come to ask if you know where Frank is? I will explain that Melia has run away and that she left my father this note. I think you had better read it.'

Mrs Sherwood took the note, frowning heavily as she came to the end of it, she looked alarmed.

'Frank married? No, I cannot believe it. He would have told us. And to Amelia? Well, a prettier girl I never saw and they seemed devoted to each other I would say, but gone off and got married without telling anyone? I won't have it.'

'You have met Melia then, Mrs Sherwood' Stephen asked.

'Yes, a little while back. Came over in Frank's trap, they did, we all had a very happy afternoon. Such a pleasant young lady and seemed very fond of Frank. But I thought it wouldn't do, with Frank being the coachman to Sir Ambrose. Not that Frank can't hold up his head with the best, we may be farmers here at Prospect, but the land has been ours for generations.' She paused and looked at the two of them.

'It's hard to know what to say, but Frank wouldn't come into the farm, he has two older brothers who work the land with Mr Sherwood, but Frank, he wanted to go his own way. And it was always horses with him, he ran our stables and saw to all our horses, the Shires and the Hunters as well as what we call the jobbing horses. He did it from being a young lad and when Sir Ambrose wanted him as coachman, he was over the moon as the saying goes.

'Mr Sherwood has been an acquaintance of Sir Ambrose for as long as I can remember.' The farmer's wife paused again. 'I'm sorry, Mr Wilkes, Miss Flintoff, I seem to be going on a bit, I don't really know how I can help you. I imagine that Amelia's father does not approve of her marrying a coachman.'

'My father thinks that Melia is far too young to be married,' said Stephen. 'She is only eighteen and he had plans for a marriage with young Welburn of Lealholme when she is a little older. Melia's mother, who died six months ago, had been fond of Frank and I think she encouraged the friendship.

'Miss Flintoff here has come to Pexton House as housekeeper and she and Melia have become good friends. We thought perhaps you would know of Frank and Melia's whereabouts, so we came as soon as we could. As you know, it is only a few miles. Can you tell us the last time you saw Frank? Has he been over here recently?'

Mrs Sherwood was shaking her head. 'We haven't seen him for over two weeks. He just popped in to tell us that Sir Ambrose had died and that he — Frank, that is — was hoping for a place as coachman elsewhere.'

Lizzie gave a sigh of relief. 'So you know where he is, Mrs Sherwood?'

'No, no, he was in such a rush and just wanted us to know that he was leaving Buckmoor Hall.'

'But didn't he say where he was going?' asked Lizzie.

'He said something about Danby, though he didn't mention the name of his new employer. Danby is not so far away and I cannot imagine that there are many landowners requiring a coachman. You would easily find him.'

Stephen stood up. 'Mrs Sherwood, how did he seem when he came to see you?'

Mrs Sherwood smiled. 'He was his usual thoughtful self and very cheerful. He just wanted to let us know that he was on the move, he is sure to send us a message when he is settled.'

'And what do you think about Melia's message to her father?'

The farmer's wife shook her head. 'I haven't been much help, have I? You must be very worried about Amelia. But it would not be like Frank to go off and get married without telling us, that is not like him at all. I feel very concerned and I can imagine that her father must be very worried.

'The best thing to do I should think is to go and see if she is anywhere in Danby. If she is with Frank then I must hope that he has done the right thing by her. I don't know what else to say.'

She bade them goodbye and they drove away from the farmhouse in silence. Lizzie glanced up at Stephen.

He looked stern and preoccupied so she did not disturb his thoughts.

As they entered Glaisdale End, he turned to her at last. 'I'm sorry, Lizzie, I've been trying to work out the best thing to do. Now we are back in Glaisdale, I think the most sensible thing is not to return to Pexton House, but to go straight over to Danby. I will risk the rough track over the moor from here to Houlsyke and then it's only a mile or two farther on to Danby. Is that all right with you? We will find a hostelry in Danby for some lunch.'

Lizzie was agreeable. 'I think we can assume that Louisa is with your father, the sooner we get to Danby the better. Let's hope we'll find them there.'

At any other time, Lizzie would have been thrilled with the ride. She loved going over the moor above Lealholme and then she had to hold on tight as they went down the steep hill into the little village of Houlsyke. After that it was easy; a good road which followed the River Esk the few miles into Danby.

'I think the Duke of Wellington is the biggest inn, we will stop for some luncheon and I can make enquiries of the landlord. He is sure to know all the big houses around the village.'

They were served with a plate of ham and some crisp and freshly-baked rolls, they both had a tankard of ale.

'Well sir,' the landlord said in a friendly voice. 'I think you're best to start trying at Ainthorpe Grange, that's Sir Percy Kelloe's place and it's between here and Ainthorpe, I'll put you in the right direction. Sir Percy keeps a carriage and several horses though I can't say as I've heard he's taken on a new coachman.

'The only other person to keep a carriage is old Mr Dursley of Park Farm, that's not so far from here. He's a nice old gentleman and he's had a coachman for years. That's all in Danby itself. There's the Old Manor, but it's nearer to Castleton, but I suppose you could try. I've done me best sir, and I wish you luck.'

* ★ *

Three hours later and after four fruit-
less visits to various country houses,
they were back in Danby. Lizzie had
spotted a baker's shop and they bought
some teacakes which the baker's young
daughter kindly buttered for them.

Then Stephen drove the trap to the
side of the river where they had their
refreshment and talked over their
disappointment at finding no trace of
Frank Sherwood or Melia.

'You look tired, Lizzie,' said Stephen
and his voice was soft.

She looked at him. 'I think it is
disappointment rather than tiredness,
Stephen. Whatever shall we do next? We
have drawn a blank here.'

He was thoughtful. 'There is some
kind of mystery about it if Frank
mentioned Danby to his mother. I
don't quite know what to think and I
feel reluctant to have to go home to
Father and confess failure, but I
suppose that is what we must do. He

116

will be getting in a worry about us in any case. Then I suppose all we can do is to wait until we hear from Melia again, or from Frank himself, she said he would write to Father. By that time they will probably be married.

'She always was a little madam and determined to have her own way. I can't help but wonder if perhaps Frank Sherwood might not suit her if she really loves him. I was very impressed with Mrs Sherwood and the fact that they did not press him into farming when it was not his choice. He obviously made an admirable coachman if Sir Ambrose was pleased with him, a more particular gentleman it would have been hard to find . . . '

He stopped speaking and turned to her, taking her hand in his. Their previous disagreement had been forgotten and they had found companionship in their useless enquiries of the afternoon.

'Lizzie, let us have a walk by the river before we return to Glaisdale. We've had a difficult day and I think we deserve a little respite before we have to face Father and Louisa. I wonder how they are getting along together?'

Lizzie gave a chuckle as he helped her down from the trap. 'That is a strange thing to say, Stephen.'

'I know that,' he seemed to agree. 'My mind seems to be in a turmoil, Melia is missing, I have been offered a senior post at the museum, I don't want to marry Louisa but perhaps I must, and here I am standing by the River Esk with your hand in mine. Do you remember we stood by the water before, Lizzie?'

Lizzie had the vivid remembrance of crossing the beck by the stepping-stones and falling into Stephen's arms. She had loved him then, she knew that she loved him now, but it seemed as though Louisa French was winning. Stephen Wilkes was never to be for Elizabeth Flintoff. But she must make some reply to him.

'I am not going to cross the stones

over the river if that is what you are thinking,' she said as lightly as she could.

'No, I was not thinking that,' he murmured. 'I was thinking that I would like to kiss you.'

Lizzie's voice rose in a sudden anger. 'How dare you. A moment ago, you were saying that you must marry Louisa. Are you that fickle? And how can you talk about kissing when you knocked poor Jimmy down because he was trying to kiss me? I don't understand you, Stephen Wilkes.'

He grinned at her, they were standing very close and looking at each other instead of at the tumbling waters. 'It is difficult, isn't it, Lizzie? I thought my life was settled. My work in York, my research at home and just the decision to make about Louisa. Then suddenly a girl from my past appears and nothing has gone right since . . . '

'Stephen!' she shrieked.

'Don't interrupt. Melia runs off to wed her coachman, I have to make up my mind about Louisa and all I want to do is to kiss my father's housekeeper. What are you laughing at?'

'You,' Lizzie replied. 'I am laughing at you. No-one would believe that you were a scholar of twenty-seven years of age. You are behaving just like Jimmy.'

He put his arm around her shoulders. 'I will have my kiss for that, and you can think of it as a thank-you kiss for all the help you have given me today. Lift your head.'

Lizzie obeyed without thinking; she was caught in a light-hearted, foolish mood. Their lips met and lingered for a long moment; there was no passion, just a sweet tenderness. She was entranced and knew she shouldn't be.

'Thank you, Lizzie.' Stephen broke the spell. 'That was very nice. Now we must go home and do some serious thinking; we are no nearer to finding Melia and a whole day has gone by.'

Lizzie was glad of those words for they stopped her from wishing that the kiss could have continued, from wishing that it could have been the first of many kisses when it had to be the last.

As she sat beside Stephen again and they set off for Glaisdale, a sudden thought came to her. 'Stephen, it is possible that your father might have had another note from Melia, had you thought of that?'

He nodded and gave the reins a little shake to hurry the horse along the lane. 'Yes, it has occurred to me. Although it was wrong of Melia to run off to be married, I do not believe that she is a hard-hearted girl. She would not want to cause Father any anxiety. We don't know the whole story, but it seems an unusual step for Frank to have taken from what his mother told us. We will go as quickly as we can and find out what Father has to say.'

At Pexton House, they found Mr Wilkes and Louisa together in the drawing-room enjoying a game of cards. Louisa looked relaxed and happy and James was in a good mood.

Lizzie was surprised and felt a little

put out, especially when Mr Wilkes greeted them quite cheerfully.

'Well, have you found the naughty girl? I see she is not with you. Sit down and tell us all about it. Louisa has been such a comfort to me, we even went for a walk down to the beck this afternoon.'

Lizzie's eyes met Stephen's and she could see the amusement there. She knew that, he too, was wondering if they had exchanged kisses.

But Stephen did not sound amused when he spoke. 'Father, we have spent the whole day chasing after Melia and Frank. Mrs Sherwood was most concerned and helpful, and I have to tell you, Father, that Melia could do a lot worse than marry a son of the Sherwoods of Egton Bridge.'

'But Frank is a coachman,' objected his father.

'He is only a coachman because that is what he chose to do, he could have had a share in the farm. But the mystery remains as to his present whereabouts and if, indeed, he is with

Melia, even married to her.

'Mrs Sherwood said that he mentioned going to Danby and we have spent the whole afternoon visiting the country houses around Danby with no success. We are at our wits end. We were hoping that Melia might have sent you another message, she must know that you would be worried about her.'

'No, there has been nothing, Stephen, but I do think . . . '

Louisa suddenly broke into the conversation. 'I am sorry to interrupt, James, but I have thought of something.' She turned to Stephen. 'Tell me, what did Mrs Sherwood actually say about Danby?'

Stephen looked at Lizzie. 'Can you remember exactly, Lizzie? I had the impression that Frank had told her that he had found a position in Danby.'

Lizzie cast her mind back to the scene in the Sherwood farmhouse. 'She said that he had been to see them to tell them that he had left Buckmoor Hall and had got another place and I think her actual words were, 'he said something about Danby though he didn't mention the name of his new employer. Why do you ask, Louisa?'

Louisa looked grave. 'I hope you will not think I am silly, but I have had a thought. You have searched all over Danby and not found Frank at any of the big houses, but the notion has come into my mind that perhaps it is the person called Danby you should be looking for and not the place.'

They all stared at her and it was Stephen who spoke first. 'Whatever do you mean, Louisa?'

She smiled. 'It may be a foolish idea, but is it not possible that it is Lord Danby you should be looking for?'

'Lord Danby?' Stephen echoed.

'Yes, he was a friend of Father's. Lord Danby, Earl of Kildale, he has a big place beyond Castleton, between Commondale and Kildale villages, I believe. What is it, Lizzie?'

Lizzie had jumped up in excitement. 'Louisa, you could be right. Oh, why didn't I think of it? There was a Lord Danby who bought some beautiful pieces of jet jewellery for his wife. Father used to send out a selection for him to choose from. He didn't come into the shop himself. I remember it being sent to Kildale.'

She turned to Stephen with great eagerness. 'Perhaps Frank was meaning that he was going as coachman to Lord Danby when he spoke to his mother and she didn't quite hear him properly. Stephen, we could go there tomorrow, what do you think?'

Stephen was speaking to Louisa. 'That was clever thinking on your part, Louisa, thank you very much. I certainly do think that it is worth a try, Lizzie. It's a few miles further along the road we were on today when we went to Danby. Shall we do it, Father? What do you think?'

Mr Wilkes was enthusiastic. 'It is possible that Melia might send us a message tomorrow — good gracious, it will be Sunday — but I'd be very grateful to you and Lizzie. I will order some supper now and if you wouldn't mind accompanying Louisa back to Buckmoor Hall, Stephen, we will all have an early night.'

Stephen decided to ride in the trap with Louisa and then to walk back to Pexton House. After their frustrating day, he felt the need for exercise and the time to himself to think about his future life.

It seemed that Louisa, also, had some thinking to do and she drove along with a lot of questions to ask of Stephen. She was dressed, very flatteringly, in a coat of stiff silk of a deep crimson. She sat up very straight with the reins in her hands. Stephen was happy to let her drive the short distance, Louisa was an excellent horsewoman.

'Does it really bother you, Stephen, if indeed Melia has married Frank Sherwood?'

He was direct in his reply. 'No, I think not. I know that it came as a shock to Father for he had planned

126

something better for her. Also, it was the way she had been underhand and had said nothing of her plans until they had been accomplished. Louisa, you must understand that the Wilkes are not at the forefront of county families.

'Father has done well and is to be admired, but his origins were humble enough though not low-bred. Melia's happiness must come first and not her place in society. From what I have known of Frank Sherwood, I would say that he is a splendidly upright young man, and his background is as good as the Wilkes any day, if not better. What do you think?'

She replied quickly and seemed sincere. 'I am inclined to agree with you about Frank, but I really do think it was naughty of Melia to run off and give James that scare. He has recovered today fortunately, but it could have been more serious. And look what trouble it has caused you and Lizzie.' She paused and glanced at him. 'Do you like Lizzie, Stephen?'

Stephen looked across at her, but her face bore the same serious expression and he was mystified by the question. He knew at the bottom of his heart what his feelings for Lizzie were, but there were too many factors preventing him from giving free rein to his emotions. And not the least was his supposed betrothal to Louisa which was why the question puzzled him.

'I have known Lizzie since she was a little girl and I have always been fond of her. It has been a pleasure for me to meet up with her again now she is a young lady. I cannot begin to tell you of her patience and encouragement today when we were searching for Melia. Why do you ask?'

'I had the feeling that Lizzie liked you very much,' she replied. They had reached the Hall and Louisa stopped the trap at the stables. 'And I wondered where it was leading.'

'It can lead nowhere. You know very well that Father wishes to marry Lizzie though I consider that she is too young for him. And, Louisa, have you forgotten our intention to marry? What of that?'

'It was never a formal betrothal and I no longer wish for it.'

'You don't want to marry me?' Stephen was astounded after years of hearing her declaring her devotion to him.

'No, I wish to marry your father.'

If Louisa had told him that she wished to journey to the moon, Stephen could not have been more astonished. He had handed her down from the trap and when she made her extraordinary statement, he held on to her hands. But immediately, Louisa snatched her hands from his grasp.

'What in the devil's name are you talking about?' he asked.

'There is no need for you to swear at me, Stephen, and I thought my statement was clear enough.'

'Has Father asked you to marry him?'

'No, he has not and neither does he

know of my regard for him. I think he still has it in mind to marry Lizzie as you have said. I agree with you that she is too young. Lizzie knows it too, for she came to Pexton House as his housekeeper and not as his wife.'

Stephen was staring at this new Louisa, she seemed suddenly older, more decided in her views. Previously, her conversation had been solely of her regard for him and how they would marry if anything happened to her father. 'Louisa, let us get this straight. I am supposed to marry you, Father wanted to marry Lizzie, now you are turning things around. You no longer wish to marry me?'

'No, I was aware that your heart was not set on the match and it has taken a day in James's company for me to realise what a wonderful gentleman he is. We are much better suited than you and I would ever have been.'

Stephen laughed then. 'So that is why you asked me if I liked Lizzie? You had it all worked out. You could marry

Father and I could marry Lizzie and everyone would be well suited.'

Louisa smiled at last. 'You are quite right, Stephen. I will say goodnight and leave you to walk back to Pexton House.'

And Stephen did just that, the conversation with Louisa ringing in his ears. He had a lot to think about.

7

Stephen and Lizzie set off for Commondale the next morning as soon as they had finished breakfast. They had to miss morning service, but as Stephen said, they would be arriving at Kildale Park, Lord Danby's country seat, when the family — and the coachman — would have returned from church.

They chatted quietly with Melia and Frank uppermost in their minds, but Stephen could not resist the opportunity of telling Lizzie of Louisa's surprising revelations of the previous evening. He went about it in a roundabout way.

'Lizzie, do you think that my father still wishes to marry you?'

She looked at him thinking it a surprising question. 'Why no,' she replied honestly. 'I think he has forgotten that he ever asked me. He has never said another word about it and I think he accepts that I am just the housekeeper. In any case, I have the feeling that he is looking towards Louisa . . . Stephen, what have I said?' she asked him for he had burst into hearty laughter.

'It is amusing, Lizzie, I must tell you what Louisa said to me when I took her home last night.'

'She still wants to marry you?'

'No, she does not. She tells me that it is Father she wishes to marry.'

'Louisa wants to marry Uncle Jack?' Lizzie could not hide her astonishment. 'But, Stephen, from what your father has told me, Louisa has been hoping to marry you for a very long time.'

'Yes, that is quite true, but she has suddenly decided that Father would suit her better. And what Louisa wants, she usually gets! Now it is you who are laughing, what is it?'

Lizzie smiled. 'It is rather strange in a way because I have been thinking how well suited they were. But what about you? Do you mind if Louisa marries your father instead of you?'

'I do not, you know how reluctant I was. In any case, I have other ideas and I have to sort out my career before I do anything else. We will have to wait and see how Louisa goes abut wooing father and what he makes of it all. He may still prefer the lovely young Miss Elizabeth Flintoff as his bride.'

Lizzie looked put out. 'Stephen Wilkes, in the first place, Miss Elizabeth Flintoff has already refused to marry her Uncle Jack, and secondly, she can never be described as lovely.'

Stephen looked down at her. She wore again her cream-coloured bonnet and her face was fresh and young and appealing. Lizzie was very desirable.

'Now we must concentrate on the task in hand. We will stop in Danby and I will ask for directions to Kildale Park from the good landlord of the Duke of Wellington Inn.'

It was not very long before they had passed through the next village which was Castleton and climbed the moor towards Commondale.

Once they were on the drive up to the big house, Lizzie began to feel nervous, wondering what they were going to find if indeed, Frank and Melia would be there.

She was not kept in suspense for very long, for in front of them, a carriage had stopped at the imposing porch and the coachman had jumped down to assist the lady and gentleman who, Lizzie thought, must be Lord and Lady Danby. She looked at Stephen and saw that he was frowning.

'That's Frank all right. Let's wait until he goes round to the stables.'

They waited for many minutes until Lizzie saw the young man emerge from the stables and start walking towards a fine-looking cottage not far away. It was built in the same stone as the big house and was neat and elegant.

'Here we go,' muttered Stephen and drove up to the cottage. He jumped down from the trap as Frank Sherwood, for indeed it was he, reached the gate.

'Frank,' Stephen called, but not unpleasantly.

'Mr Wilkes,' said the surprised Frank looking flustered. 'However did you find us?'

But Stephen had no time to reply as the front door was opened and a very pretty and excited Melia came running down the path towards them.

Lizzie had jumped down from the trap and met Melia at the gate. 'Melia, you are here, you wicked little girl. What do you mean by it? And are you and Frank really married?'

'Lizzie, Lizzie, how can you possibly be here so quickly? Frank sent the letter to Papa soon after breakfast this morning before he took Lord and Lady Danby to morning service . . . oh, it is so exciting. Yes, we are married and have the most lovely little house, and I have a maid and please come in and we will have some tea. And you will stay for luncheon. Patsy — she is my maid — does the cooking as well. I am so lucky. And you must tell me how you found us.'

Frank and Stephen had joined them and Frank put an arm round Melia's shoulders. 'Stop chattering, Melia, and show our guests into the parlour. We have a lot of explaining to do.'

Stephen walked into the house with Lizzie, his hand on her arm, a whisper in her ear. 'I think we have found a happily married couple, Lizzie, we must listen to their story. They seem so excited and this is such a splendid place, it will be hard to be cross with Melia.'

They all drank tea and Melia was obviously eager to make the explanations. Lizzie discovered Frank to be a very serious and good-looking man and obviously a very proud one.

Melia launched into her story and for the moment, lost her skittishness. 'Stephen and Lizzie, it is good of you to come all this way to make sure that I was all right. And you can stop worrying on Papa's account, for by now he will have received the letter Frank has written to him.'

She looked from one to the other. 'Now, I must tell you why it was I had to run away, and it is only fair to warn you that it is a long, long story and I don't mind if you interrupt.'

Stephen looked serious. 'There will be a lot of questions to be answered, Melia.'

She nodded. 'Yes, I know that, but some things you know already. You know that Frank and I have been close friends for a long time, but it is only this last year that we realised that we loved each other truly and wanted to marry. But Papa did not approve, I begged and begged him but he would have none of it. That was because Frank was the coachman to Sir Ambrose and Papa had plans for me to marry that Welburn of Lealholme. I have never even liked the gentleman and he is much older than me.'

Frank broke into the story. 'I was not going to marry Melia unless she had her father's permission, and I intended to wait until I had a better place. I would not have left Sir Ambrose, he was very good to me.'

Melia nodded. 'So when Frank was offered to be coachman to Lord Danby, he was in a quandary. He said he would think about it. Well, I like to think that fate was on his side, because poor Sir Ambrose died and Louisa dismissed Frank the same day. I thought that was very hard of her, but then I always did think she was a hard person.' She looked at Stephen. 'I am sorry, Stephen, I was forgetting that you were going to marry her.'

He grinned. 'I think that possibility is a thing of the past, Melia, please continue with your story.'

'Frank went straight to Lord Danby and obtained the position as head coachman — it is a large stables here — but that is where the trouble started. You see Lord Danby wanted Frank, but he had always insisted that his coachman lived in this house and that he was married, so that his wife could keep the house in order. You must see that it is very comfortably furnished.'

They looked around them and Lizzie thought that the furniture and furnishings of the parlour were superior to those of Pexton House. She could understand Lord Danby being particular. 'It's a lovely room, Melia,' she said.

'The whole house is like this. It is a thing with Lord Danby that his servants must be as comfortable as he is himself. To go back to the story, Frank didn't know what to do, but he told Lord Danby that he was planning to be married soon. That was a lie, of course, but everything depended on it and he was so taken with the stables and this house, he came back to ask me what we should do. He wanted to ask Papa.'

'Why didn't he?' asked Stephen.

'I wouldn't let him. At best, I knew that Papa would only say that I was to wait until I was twenty-one and that wouldn't do at all. So I thought hard and I'm afraid I played Frank a trick, but he has forgiven me.' Melia flashed a smile at her new husband.

She is very happy, thought Lizzie, but she didn't say anything.

Melia continued. 'I worked it out for myself and in the end, Frank agreed. I told him to get a licence for us to be married in the church in Kildale — I knew that if you were resident in a place for fifteen days you could be married in the church and that you didn't have to have the banns called. Then I told Frank to tell Lord Danby he was about to be married and that he had left his old position and could start at Kildale Park straight away if that was acceptable. He would take good care of the house until his wife joined him.

'Lord Danby wished to know who the young lady was and when he learned that she was Miss Wilkes, the daughter of James Wilkes of Pexton House in Glaisdale, he was very pleased and agreed immediately to take Frank on as his coachman.'

Frank could not stop himself from interrupting. 'She is a managing little madam,' he said with a grin. 'But I made her promise to tell her father of the situation and the whole family could come for the wedding.'

'And so you left Glaisdale and took up your new position. Did you go and see your parents?' Stephen asked though he knew what the answer was going to be.

'Yes, I saw Mother but not Father and I told her that I had left Sir Ambrose and had a new place with Lord Danby . . . what is it?'

He was looking at Stephen and Lizzie for they had both burst into loud laughter. It was Stephen who told the tale of how Mrs Sherwood had caught only the name of Danby and how they had spent the previous day on a wild goose chase in and around that village.

'But, Frank,' continued Stephen. 'I still don't quite understand. Why did Melia have to run away?'

'I don't know how to tell you, I was so angry. I had started my work here and had been over to Glaisdale and Melia and I had met twice. She told me that she was still hoping to persuade her father and that I was to fix up the wedding for yesterday.

'Well, Friday evening came and there was Patsy baking and preparing food for the wedding breakfast. The wedding in the church was fixed for three o'clock the following day . . . ' he broke off and looked uncomfortable. 'I don't know how to tell you the next part. You can guess what happened for she left Mr Wilkes the note.'

'Melia arrived,' said Lizzie and turned to the young girl. 'Melia, you never rode over here on you own with just your silver brush and comb set and your favourite doll.'

'And my wedding dress,' said Melia, she still looked happy and not in the least penitent. 'At least, it was my best party dress, but it was of ivory satin so I thought it would do. I rode all that way on my pony with just one bag to carry. It seemed to take hours, but I found Kildale Park easily enough and then Frank. He was furiously angry. I was scared. I didn't know he could be so angry, he has always been so kind and loving. But when he found out that I hadn't asked Father and just left a note, he was furious. But I started to cry because I thought he didn't want me and he would take me straight back to Glaisdale in his trap. But I refused to go, so we talked it over and he said that as his position depended on him having a wife, we'd better go through with it even if none of the family were present.'

Lizzie had an alarming thought and hastily interrupted. 'But, Melia, you never stayed here in this house the night before you were married?'

'I spent the night over the stables and left Melia here with Patsy, so it was all very proper,' Frank said.

'And what about the wedding?' asked Lizzie. 'You had no guests.'

'Yes, we did,' replied Melia promptly.

'Patsy was ever so good. She cooked us a lunch, but I was too excited to eat. Then she fetched two of the servants from the big house and the undergardener and we all went to Kildale Church which is down near the railway station. They walked and Frank took me in the trap and he said I looked beautiful.'

'You've forgotten something, Melia,' said Frank suddenly.

'Oh, yes. In the middle of all the celebrating, Lord and Lady Danby appeared and although they were shocked that I didn't have any of my family there, they seemed pleased with me and congratulated Frank on his choice of bride.' Melia looked at Stephen and Lizzie. 'And that's all except, as I told you, Frank insisted on sending a letter with one of the stable boys to tell Papa that we were married. So you will tell Papa all about it, won't you, Lizzie? I am sure if he knew how happy I am, he would forgive me.'

It was Frank's turn to speak. 'He will have received my letter this morning, so

I hope he won't think too badly of me. Tell him that I will bring Melia to see him on my very first free day. I hope that he has recovered from his upset, I expect Miss Louisa will have stayed with him while you have been coming here.'

* ★ *

Louisa was indeed at Pexton House, she had accompanied James to morning service for he said he had recovered sufficiently. When they returned from the church in Glaisdale End for their luncheon, they found that a letter had been brought over from Kildale Park in their absence.

James ordered sherry for them and they sat together in the drawing-room, while he opened the letter and glanced at its contents.

'Well, goodness me, it is a letter from Frank and a more nicely written and polite letter I have never received. You had better read it, Louisa, my dear.'

Louisa took it from him.

Dear Mr Wilkes,

I am sure that Melia's running away from home will have caused you much anxiety and I write to apologise on her behalf.

I must tell you that it was never my intention to marry Melia in an underhand way. My position as head-coachman here at Kildale Park required that I was married so I obtained a licence and left it to Melia to obtain your permission and to ask you all to the wedding.

However, it seems that Melia was afraid to tell you of our plans and she arrived here unannounced on Friday.

I have a substantial and well-furnished house provided with my position and it will make us a good home. We look forward to seeing you here and I will bring Melia to see you on my first free day.

Yours sincerely,
Frank Sherwood.

'Frank has said everything that needed to be said. He is an estimable young man and my father thought the world of him. I am pleased to think that he is now Lord Danby's coachman.' Louisa looked at him. His face wore a little frown and she knew what it meant. 'You will have to forgive Melia and wish her well, James, she is obviously very happy.'

He smiled then. 'You are right, Louisa, you know Frank better than I do. Rhoda and I spoiled Melia, I suppose because she was our only daughter and you have to admit to her being a very pretty young miss.

'I can begin to feel my old self again. That's thanks to you, Louisa. You have been most punctilious in your attentions to me since yesterday morning and I am more than grateful to you.' He stopped thoughtfully. 'Now, as soon as your period of mourning permits, you will be arranging your marriage to Stephen. It will be strange to have you as a daughter.'

Louisa took a deep breath, she knew of her intentions and now was the time to act. 'I am not going to marry Stephen and I have told him so.'

He sat up straight, then leaned forward and touched her hand. 'You are not going to marry Stephen? But it has been expected all this time.'

'Yes, I do know that, but the events of these last few days have caused me to change my mind,' she said coolly and then watched his face. 'I would like to marry you, James.'

She thought his expression comical and she knew that her plan would succeed. His good-looking face turned red and he started to bluster, then he stared hard at her and his natural colour returned. He nodded twice, then smiled in delight.

'Louisa, my dearest girl, what are you saying? You are very forthright, but then that is your nature. But there is something wrong.' He paused and gave a chuckle. Then he leaned forward and took her hand in his. 'I should be asking you if you would do me the honour of becoming my wife. I have not even given it a thought before because I knew that you were attached to Stephen. It seems I am wrong. You will marry me, Louisa?'

Louisa was all smiles. 'Thank you, James, I gladly accept your offer. I suddenly realised that Stephen was far too young for me. He would do better for Lizzie.

'Lizzie turned you down, James, and that is why she is here as your housekeeper. I believe her to be in love with Stephen, but I am not sure of his feelings for her. We will have to wait and see.' Louisa had let her hands lie in James's clasp, something she would never have allowed Stephen. 'And now do you mind if we talk of our plans?'

'So how long do you think we should wait until we can become man and wife?'

Louisa knew exactly. 'I think three months would suffice, perhaps we could be married in September. Would that be agreeable to you?'

He gave a beaming smile. 'I could wish it were sooner, my dear. Do you think I might kiss you?'

For the first time, Louisa hesitated, then she offered him her cheek and flushed deep crimson as his lips touched her face.'

'I never allowed Stephen to kiss me,' she said primly. 'You are honoured. Now we must talk business, James.'

'Talk business? Whatever do you mean? We have agreed to be married and you say we must talk about business? That is a strange thing for a young lady to say.'

'I am not a silly young thing, James, and Father was ailing for such a long time that I learned to run the affairs of Buckmoor Hall for him. I know that we have a good steward in Mr Easterbrook, but not everything can be left to one's steward.'

'Louisa, what are you saying? You know that if you married me that Pexton House would become your home.'

'I think not, James.'

'My goodness gracious, Louisa, this is my house. You are not supposing that I could leave it for Buckmoor Hall, are you?' It was not like James Wilkes to bluster, but this admirable young woman whom he had just asked to be his wife, was plunging him into uncertainties.

Louisa leaned forward in her chair, smiled and took one of his hands in hers, 'James, I must speak plainly. I am a very wealthy young lady and not only that, I have inherited Buckmoor Hall and its estate. I have lived there all my life and I would like to see it continue to prosper. I believe that you and I together would be able to do that splendidly. Yes, I am asking you to give up Pexton House, but it is in my mind that Stephen would benefit from the arrangement. He will inherit it one day. In any case, I see no harm in you handing it over to him before that when he needs it most. On his marriage, perhaps.'

The owner of Pexton House got up and walked about the room in some agitation. He would not admit to himself that he loved Louisa, but he did admire her. He had never been sure that she would have made Stephen a good wife because of their age difference. She almost was nearer to him than she was to Stephen.

But here she was and with great determination trying to change his ways. Buckmoor Hall his? He had never dreamed of such affluence. When he had inherited Pexton House after Cicely had died, he had considered that he had done well, and he had been happy there.

He paused to look out of the window and Louisa came up to him, it was almost as though she had read his thoughts. Her voice was suddenly gentle. 'I know you have been happy here, James, but you are not on your own now. Think how contented the two of us would be together at Buckmoor, you have always liked the house and there would be no loneliness for either of us.'

He looked down at her, struck by her composure and the kindness of her expression. He had never thought of Louisa French as being a kind person, but perhaps he had misjudged her.

Putting his hands on her shoulders, he looked at her and saw a future of wealth and comfort. It beckoned him.

'Louisa, I do believe you are right and it would please me to give Pexton House to Stephen. All the time he was hesitating about marrying you, I was vexed with him, but I do believe he has done me a good turn. Heavens, if I won't kiss you again!'

8

Stephen and Lizzie opened the door upon this scene in the drawing-room at Pexton House that Sunday afternoon. They stood in the doorway transfixed and Stephen grasped Lizzie's arm. 'Father, Louisa,' he said and there was a shocked astonishment in his voice.

James, his hands still on Louisa's shoulders, looked round and smiled. 'Stephen and Lizzie, you have arrived at a very opportune moment. Louisa has agreed to marry me and we have just had a business discussion. I hope you will congratulate us, I will send for some champagne. Come in.'

Lizzie went forward, kissed Mr Wilkes and shook hands with Louisa; Stephen shook hands with them both and offered his congratulations.

'I am very pleased,' he said and there was real joy in his voice. 'I hesitated too long over us, Louisa, and now you have won Father. That is splendid.'

'What is even more splendid, Stephen,' said his father, 'is that Louisa and I will take up residence at Buckmoor Hall and I can hand Pexton House over to you.'

Lizzie felt Stephen stiffen and guessed that this last piece of news had added to the complication of Stephen's plans for his future career. But she had no time to consider the implications for Mr Wilkes was demanding to hear all the news about Melia and Frank.

'So did you find them at Kildale Park? They will have told you that Frank sent a letter to me, I'll show it to you, I couldn't have written a more considerate letter myself. I'm most impressed by the young man. But sit down, here is the champagne and we now have a double celebration. Melia and Frank, and now Louisa and myself. Now you must tell us all about their house and if Melia is happy.'

A lot of talking was done that

afternoon and Lizzie was included as though she was one of the family.

After dinner, James and Louisa went over to Buckmoor Hall and Stephen asked Lizzie to walk down to the beck with him.

They did not cross the stepping-stones, but strolled along the edge of the water until they reached the point where the beck joined the Buckmoor estate.

'Are you pleased about your father and Louisa?' Lizzie asked.

'Yes, I am,' Stephen replied. 'It was what Louisa wanted and she seems to have cajoled Father into thinking that it is what he wants, too. I hope you had not been planning to marry him yourself, Lizzie.'

She laughed merrily. 'I would have said yes in the first place and I have been happy here at Pexton House as housekeeper, but I suppose that everything will change now.'

'In a little while,' said Stephen distantly. 'It will be splendid to be the owner of Pexton House, but I am not sure if it is what I want at the moment. I can't talk about it, Lizzie, it is too complicated and it is all tied up with the museum, as you probably know. I have to make some big decisions and there are a lot of things unresolved.'

Am I one of those things thought Lizzie sadly. I do love him, but I have not the least idea of his feelings for me. These last two days have been out of the ordinary and there has been no time to consider ourselves. All I know now is that Stephen is free of Louisa, free to go his own way.

Before returning to the house, they paused at the stepping stones and Stephen smiled suddenly. He had been very serious the whole evening.

'I will go back to York with the memory of you crossing the stones and falling into my arms. I wonder if that is where you belong?' And with these strange words, he pulled her close to him and kissed her. He had kissed her before, but not like this. His lips sought hers in passion, and with a wave of feeling, Lizzie returned the kiss as he held her closer and closer.

Then suddenly she was free, standing on her own.

He took a long look at her and his words reached her. 'I like you very much, Lizzie.'

Then he turned away and went striding over the field leaving Lizzie standing by the beck, shaken and bewildered by his behaviour.

★ ★ ★

Next morning, he drove off early. He said goodbye coldly as he reached the front door. 'I do not expect to be back at Pexton House for some weeks. Goodbye, Lizzie.'

For the rest of that day, Lizzie set about her tasks, but she did so miserably. Those last words of Stephen's at the beck echoed round and round in her mind. 'I like you very much, Lizzie.'

Had she been wrong in thinking that

his kiss had told her more than that? She knew she had loved him from the beginning, but at first it had been a hopeless love because of Louisa. Now, Louisa was out of the picture, but — and Lizzie kept saying this to herself — was it so wrong of her to think that Stephen might turn to her? It must be so. She had been mistaken in the kisses and had nurtured a foolish hope. Now she must return to a life without Stephen and with an upset in the household when Mr Wilkes and Louisa were married and removed to Buckmoor Hall.

But, for Lizzie, that upset was to come much sooner than she had expected. In fact, it came the following morning.

On the day of Stephen's departure for York, Lizzie noticed that Louisa was closeted in the library with Mr Wilkes for almost the whole day. They even ate their luncheon there. Lizzie thought nothing of it as she knew very well that there would be a lot of arrangements for the couple to make.

The following morning, Lizzie herself was summoned to the library and she went into the room with an eagerness to learn what had been decided between the newly-betrothed pair.

One look at James Wilkes' face told her that all was not well. Surely he and Louisa had not quarrelled already, she said to herself.

'Sit down, Lizzie. I have an unpleasant task to perform, but first I will make some explanations.'

Lizzie did sit down, not understanding anything.

'You will have been aware,' Mr Wilkes went on, 'that Louisa and I had a long discussion yesterday. We came to a decision and it is going to make a lot of difference to the household. Louisa feels the need of a gentleman to help her at Buckmoor Hall, so we have agreed that I will leave Pexton House and move to the hall straight away. Louisa has a housekeeper and Jimmy will be home this week, so the properties will be observed.

'We know that our marriage cannot decently take place until September.' He paused and looked uncomfortable. 'I am sorry, Lizzie, but I am keeping Mrs Hamlyn at Pexton House for Stephen, but it is necessary for me to ask you to leave straight away. There will be no need for a housekeeper with the house lying empty.'

Lizzie listened as in a dream. Leave Pexton House tomorrow? But where could she go?

She said just that to Mr Wilkes, who stood very formally in front of her. She seemed to have lost her nice Uncle Jack and she suspected Louisa's influence in all this.

'But where can I go,' she asked and then felt feeble.

He looked surprised and smiled for the first time. 'But you have your parents still in Whitby, you will be able to go home. I am sorry this is all so sudden, Lizzie, but Louisa's wishes must come first with me now.

'I am very grateful for all the good work you have done here and I will miss you, but once we have decided to marry, Louisa and I had to go ahead with our plans. Please give my regards to your mother and father and I hope you find them well.'

Lizzie sat stony-faced and stony-hearted. She was not going to tell James Wilkes that her father was now a fisherman living in the cramped fisherman's cottage of his brother's, where there would be no room for her. She must speak to him quickly and then go to her room.

'I have enjoyed being here, Mr Wilkes, and I am glad that you will soon be established at Buckmoor Hall. I will go and pack up my things and be ready to leave in the morning. You will send me to the station in the trap?'

'Yes, of course, Lizzie. I will say goodbye to you in the morning, I am going over to Buckmoor now. Louisa is expecting me.'

Lizzie reached her bedroom, sat on

her bed and allowed the tears to roll down her cheeks. I hadn't expected it to end like this, she thought, and I don't suppose I shall ever see Stephen again. But Stephen is gone already and the most important thing to think about is whatever I am to do with myself in Whitby? I am not going to worry Mother and Papa with my troubles, they have enough of their own.

The rest of the day passed miserably and Lizzie told only Mrs Hamlyn of her departure, letting that good lady think that she was going home to her parents.

There was only one bright spot in the day, and that was when Mr Wilkes called her to the library again and, much more like his old self, told her that he was going to give her a parting gift of £50 in lieu of notice, but not to say anything to Louisa about it.

Lizzie left the room feeling a little relieved, knowing that £50 would see her safely in a boarding house while she searched for work. And poor Uncle Jack, she thought as she left the library, he is under Louisa's thumb already.

She arrived at Whitby station clutching a large bag — she had arranged with Mrs Hamlyn to have her trunk sent off later — and feeling as though the past twenty-four hours had been a dream, almost a nightmare. One minute she had been settled at Pexton House and now here she was back in Whitby with no home and no work.

But as she stood outside the railway station and saw the harbour and the familiar streets of her childhood, her confidence came flowing back. She would not worry her parents for the time being. First of all, she would find a small hotel or boarding house and then she would search for work. The thought of Mr Wilkes gift helped her and she stepped out through the streets knowing exactly where she was going.

It had always been one of Lizzie's favourite walks to go along the west cliff and walk within sight of the sea and there, overlooking the sea, where the grand houses of North Terrace and

Royal Crescent, many of them converted into hotels for the summer visitors to Whitby. It was a popular resort, with fine sands which still had the old-fashioned bathing machines.

Lizzie first tried a small hotel on North Terrace but there were no vacancies and the proprietor told her to try Mrs Newbitt at the West Cliff Boarding House, 17 Royal Crescent. It was only just round the corner, she was told, but Lizzie knew exactly where to go.

Here she found Mrs Newbitt, a very large, smiling lady who Lizzie liked immediately.

'Yes, dear, I do have a vacancy. It is a small room at the top of the house and people don't like climbing all those stairs, but perhaps you are young enough not to mind that. Do you know Whitby?'

Lizzie told Mrs Newbitt briefly of her circumstances and found the good lady sympathetic and encouraging. She was a motherly figure and inspired confidences, but Lizzie was careful in choosing her story, though she did let it be known that she would be looking for work in Whitby.

Mrs Newbitt took her up to her room, which indeed was small, but it was not expensive and it was comfortable. There was a small high window which gave a view over Whitby, but Lizzie had to stand on tip-toe to see out of it.

There followed several frustrating days, though Lizzie blamed herself on being particular on what she chose to do. Her first choice was to go for a shop assistant, but her father's jet shop had not been the only one to fail. She tried the various drapers' shops, but found that they employed young men and boys as assistants rather than girls and young women such as herself.

She could have worked in the fish market, but found herself fastidious about handling and gutting freshly-caught fish and was ashamed of herself. She remembered her father and knew she lacked the courage to follow his example.

Lizzie afterwards thought that she would have not got through those disappointing days if it had not been for Mrs Newbitt's kindness of heart. Each day, Lizzie told her of her wanderings about Whitby and her failure.

On the fourth day, she returned to Royal Crescent dejectedly to find Mrs Newbitt full of news.

'Come into my sitting-room, Lizzie. Something has happened.'

Lizzie was amused by the air of intrigue and sat down opposite the landlady in the small but cosy sitting-room.

'What is it, Mrs Newbitt, you haven't found me a job, have you?' Despair in her heart, Lizzie tried to make a joke of it.

'I might have,' said Mrs Newbitt.

'What do you mean?' asked Lizzie curiously.

'Well, it depends on you, Lizzie. You know that Nancy of mine — always was a bit flighty, though a cheerful girl — the one that sees to all my linen. Washes it and mends and keeps it nice as you know.'

Lizzie nodded, but said nothing and Mrs Newbitt continued.

'I always suspected Nancy not to be behaving properly with that young man of hers, but I kept her on because she was a good worker. Now you can guess what's happened, Lizzie. Going to have a baby, Nancy is, and has brought shame on West Cliff Boarding House. I have dismissed her this very morning and she's gone.

'I'm not that hard-hearted, but I'm particular when it comes to morals as any chapel-going person should be. I made sure the young man will marry her and sent her off with a month's wages and a gift for the baby. What do you think of all that?'

Lizzie was rather at a loss. 'You did right, Mrs Newbitt,' was all she said.

'Well, what do you think, Lizzie? Would you like to be my new linen-maid? Oh, I know it's beneath what you've been used to, but I like you, Lizzie, and you are welcome to stay on in your little room if you will take on the linen. It's not hard work, but at this time of year, we are busy with all the visitors and I'm very particular about the linen. What do you say to it?'

Lizzie almost laughed in relief. From jeweller's daughter to housekeeper, to linen-maid. But why not? At Pexton House she had been in charge of the linen and knew what was required of a linen-maid. And she liked it at Royal Crescent, she liked Mrs Newbitt. It might be a humble job, but humility was a virtue. She made a quick decision and was grateful.

'I'll do it, Mrs Newbitt, and I must thank you for offering it to me. I know just what is needed and I'll do my best. I won't let you down.'

Mrs Newbitt smiled. 'Good, that's settled then, but Lizzie, there's one thing I insist upon.'

'What's that?' asked Lizzie. Mrs Newbitt had sounded almost stern.

'Before you start working here, you must go and see your parents. It's only fair to let them know where you are and you needn't be ashamed of working in Royal Crescent. Will you promise me?'

Lizzie smiled, how could she refuse the well-meaning Mrs Newbitt? 'I will go to Uncle George's this evening and I will start work for you in the morning straight after breakfast.'

Lizzie made her way to Cliff Street that evening. She had kept in touch with her mother by letter when she was at Pexton House, but she had not seen them since the day she had left the shop in Church Street.

Lizzie was pleased to find both her parents in good health and spirits. With the money from the sale of the jet business, Mr Flintoff had been able to buy his own fishing boat. He had taken on a partner and Lizzie was pleased to learn that they were to move into their own cottage nearby.

She surprised them with the news of James Wilkes' marriage to Miss Louisa French, but they were dismayed at her present circumstances, begging her to join them as soon as they moved. But she assured them that she was contented to be Mrs Newbitt's linen-maid and reminded them jokingly of how she had always washed the family bed-linen in the dolly tub in the wash-house at Church Street.

Lizzie went back to Royal Crescent feeling happier that she had seen them and ready to start her new work the next day.

In that first week, Lizzie enjoyed her work and also enjoyed the evenings when Mrs Newbitt insisted that Lizzie joined her in her sitting-room. They soon became good friends and bit by bit, the story of Lizzie's life and the circumstances of her leaving Pexton House were told. She made mention of Mr Stephen Wilkes and Mrs Newbitt was left to guess that here was an unfinished romance.

It would be true to say that in the days of her walking round Whitby looking for work, Lizzie had not thought of Stephen at all. But gradually, as she chatted to Mrs Newbitt, her heartache returned and she found herself wondering what Stephen had decided to do with his life and if he was still at the museum in York.

* * *

If Lizzie had been able to take a peep into the Yorkshire Museum in the grounds of St Mary's Abbey in York, she would have found a discontented Stephen Wilkes. He had not as yet, taken up his new post.

In the week which had taken Lizzie to Whitby and found her working as a linen-maid, Stephen had been busy enough during the day, but in the evenings on his own at home, he found that his mind was restlessly searching for the answer to the question of how to proceed with his life. He knew he was fortunate in the opportunities offered to him at the museum, but why did it not seem enough?

And he knew very well that Lizzie Flintoff was one of the reasons for his dilemma. He loved Lizzie. He had fallen in love with her the minute he had met up with her again even though he had been still attached to Louisa.

And their last walk together worried him. He had kissed her with all the passion he felt for her, then had told her that she 'liked her very much,' and walked away from her. He had no idea what her feelings for him were except in her response to his kiss. Dear Lizzie, he would sigh.

Then he would pull himself together and set out the options for his life. He could accept the senior post at the museum, give up all thoughts for his research, ask Lizzie to marry him and enjoy a prosperous and fashionable life in York. Or, he could break off his link with the museum, return to Pexton

House which would be his one day, and offer Lizzie a life with little money and himself away for a lot of the time visiting archaeological sites.

His answer came one evening as he walked into the Abbey Gardens, and found himself sitting on the same stones where he and Lizzie had talked the day that Melia had run away. She had been so understanding about his work and about Louisa, he could almost remember the feel of her hand in his.

I am a fool, he told himself, it is not my decision. If I want to marry Lizzie then it is necessary that I talk it over with her. We live in enlightened times, Lizzie must be allowed to say what she thinks.

Twenty-four hours later, he was driving the trap up to Pexton House. Inside the front door, he found it strangely quiet and no-one to be seen.

He made his way to the kitchen and found a woebegone Mrs Hamlyn.

She started up. 'Oh, Mr Stephen, I'm

that glad to see you. Right worried I've been.'

'Whatever is it, Mrs Hamlyn? And why is the place like a morgue? Where is Lizzie?'

'Gone.'

'Gone?' he echoed. 'Whatever do you mean? And where is Father.'

'He's gone too. Over to Buckmoor Hall along of Miss Louisa, I thought he would have written to you to tell you.'

Stephen pulled chairs up to the kitchen table and made her sit down and tell him everything.

'Blast!' he said. 'It's all Louisa's doing. And you've not heard from Lizzie?'

'No, she said she would write to me as soon as she was settled for I've still got her trunk here, but then it's only a week, after all.'

'I'll go to Whitby first thing in the morning. You think she went to her parents?'

'Yes, but she couldn't stay there because there wasn't room.'

'But they'll know where she is. And they went to live with Mr Flintoff's brother, Lizzie's Uncle George, I will find his address in Bulmers Directory, that's no problem. Call me early in the morning, Mrs Hamlyn.'

'But, I must give you some supper, Mr Stephen.'

'No, thank you, I think I will go and see Father and Louisa, I must find out how I stand.' He paused and then stooped down and kissed her on the cheek. 'Now you stop worrying. Something is telling me that maybe Lizzie and I will come and live at Pexton House.'

'Oh, Mrs Stephen, wouldn't that be lovely.'

Mrs Hamlyn had the biggest smile ever seen on her face as Stephen left the kitchen and made his way to Buckmoor Hall.

★   ★   ★

The meeting between Stephen, Louisa and his father went well. They had a discussion and parted pleasantly. Stephen with the knowledge that Pexton House was to be his and that he could offer it to Lizzie when he found her.

The directory had said, Mr George Flintoff, 19 Cliff Street, and Stephen was driving down Cliff Street by ten o'clock the next morning.

Then he was standing in front of an amazed Mrs Flintoff.

'Why, if it isn't Stephen Wilkes! It's years since I saw you, Stephen, but I'd have known you anywhere. I've never forgotten how you used to tease our Lizzie. You know she's left your father?'

'Yes, I've just come from Pexton House. I must see her, Mrs Flintoff, do you know where she is?'

He saw her frown. 'I don't know if you and your father would be very pleased, but she is linen-maid up at West Cliff Boarding House in Royal Crescent.'

'Lizzie a linen-maid? But she is a lady, Mrs Flintoff.'

'We've had to stop thinking of ladies

and gentlemen, Stephen, my Joshua is a fisherman now, and linen-maid was all Lizzie could get when she left your father.'

'I'll go after her.' He started towards the door then realised he was being rude. 'I love her, Mrs Flintoff, and I am thinking of leaving my post at the Yorkshire Museum. I want to find out if Lizzie would marry me if I am a penniless archaeologist.'

Mrs Flintoff's smile told its own story. 'I think she would marry you if you were the chimney sweep, if I know our Lizzie.'

He bent and kissed her cheek. 'Bless you,' he said.

It took Stephen only minutes to go up the hill to the West Cliff, and he stopped at number 17 Royal Crescent with a feeling of optimism.

He met Mrs Newbitt in the entrance hall. 'Can I help you, sir?' she asked, impressed with the young gentleman.

'I am Mr Stephen Wilkes and I am hoping to find Miss Lizzie Flintoff here.

I believe she is your linen-maid.'

Mrs Newbitt looked as though she could have hugged him. 'You are Mr Stephen? Well, I never, it's all come right at last. I'll fetch Lizzie.' And with these words, she hurried up the stairs.

Lizzie had been sitting mending a torn sheet in the linen-room when an excited Mrs Newbitt burst in. 'Come quick, Lizzie, if it isn't Mr Wilkes to see you.'

Uncle Jack, thought Lizzie? Whatever does he want? But she hurried down the stairs. When she saw Stephen, she could only shriek his name.

'Stephen!' she cried out and she was in his arms.

He held her very close. 'Lizzie, I've found you. Walk with me to the cliff top. You don't mind if I take Lizzie off?' he asked Mrs Newbitt.

'I am delighted,' said that smiling lady.

There was a lovely view from the cliff top in Whitby. The harbour and the ruins of the old abbey on one side, the sweep of the sands on the other, but neither were seen by Stephen and Lizzie.

'How did you find me?' she asked him. 'Why did you come?'

He gave her a hug in full view of those taking their morning stroll along North Terrace. 'Lizzie, there is so much to say, but only one thing that matters. I love you and please will you marry me.'

Her face was happy, but she was remembering their last meeting at the beck. 'You told me you liked me very much,' she said to him reproachfully.

'I was a fool, but I did not know what to do about the museum. I knew I wanted to marry you, but I did not know whether to offer you the wealth and importance of living in York society, or to live with very little money while I went off for weeks at a time. Then there was my book on the Beaker Folk . . . '

'Stephen, wait, wait. I don't even know who the Beaker Folk are . . . '

'Were, my love, were. They were our ancestors thousands of years ago.

Marry me and you can spend a lifetime learning about the Beaker Folk . . . why are you laughing?'

'Oh, Stephen, there is no-one quite like you. It must be the most wonderful proposal of marriage a girl ever had.'

He took no notice of her interruption. 'You understand what I am saying to you? I love you very much and I do want you for my wife. I am giving you the choice of fine society in York or Pexton House — which is now mine by the way — with me being away for some of the time, and not very much money.'

Tears instead of laughter came to her eyes then. 'Oh, Stephen, it is just like you to consider my wishes when it is your career that matters. But you don't like city life, do you?'

'No, now I am here, the answer is plain to me. I love you and I love Glaisdale. Is that what you would like best?'

She reached up and kissed his cheek. 'Yes, I would like it very much, Stephen.'

'So have you a reply for me?' His tone was teasing and loving at the same time.

Lizzie's voice was full of happiness. 'I do love you and I would like to marry you — Beaker Folk and all.'

'Rogue,' he said. 'I am going to kiss you, never mind who is looking.'

And he did.

THE END

We do hope that you have enjoyed reading this large print book.

Did you know that all of our titles are available for purchase?

We publish a wide range of high quality large print books including:
**Romances, Mysteries, Classics
General Fiction
Non Fiction and Westerns**

Special interest titles available in large print are:
**The Little Oxford Dictionary
Music Book, Song Book
Hymn Book, Service Book**

Also available from us courtesy of Oxford University Press:
**Young Readers' Dictionary
(large print edition)
Young Readers' Thesaurus
(large print edition)**

For further information or a free brochure, please contact us at:
**Ulverscroft Large Print Books Ltd.,
The Green, Bradgate Road, Anstey,
Leicester, LE7 7FU, England.
Tel:** (00 44) **0116 236 4325**
Fax: (00 44) **0116 234 0205**

VISIONS OF THE HEART

Christine Briscomb

When property developer Connor Grant contracted Natalie Jensen to landscape the grounds of his large country house near Ashley in South Australia, she was ecstatic. But then she discovered he was acquiring — and ripping apart — great swathes of the town. Her own mother's house and the hall where the drama group met were two of his targets. Natalie was desperate to stop Connor's plans — but she also had to fight the powerful attraction flowing between them.

DIVIDED LOYALTIES

Phyllis Demaine

When Heather's fiancé, Adrian, is offered a wonderful job in America their future seems rosy. However, Adrian's brother, Carl, a widower, asks for Heather's help with his small, deaf son. Help which, as a speech therapist, Heather is qualified to give. But things become complicated when Carl goes abroad on business and returns with Gisel, to whom his son takes an instant dislike. This puts Heather in the position of having to choose between the boy's happiness and her own.

17 ROYAL CRESCENT.
19 CLIFE STREET.